MURDER AT
PIRATE'S COVE

First in an Adorable New Series!

Ellery Page, aspiring screenwriter,
Scrabble champion, and guy-with-worst-luck-in-
the-world-when-it-comes-to-dating, is ready to
make a change. So when he learns he's
inherited both a failing bookshop and
a falling-down mansion in the quaint seaside village
of Pirate's Cove in Rhode Island,
it's full steam ahead!

Sure enough, the village is charming, its residents
amusingly eccentric, and widowed police chief Jack
Carson is decidedly yummy (though possibly as
straight as he is stern). However, the bookstore *is*
failing, the mansion *is* falling down, and there's that
little drawback of finding rival bookseller
—and head of the unwelcoming-committee—
Trevor Maples *dead* during the
annual Buccaneer Days celebration.

Still, it could be worse. And once
Police Chief Carson learns Trevor was killed
with the cutlass hanging over the door
of Ellery's bookstore, it is.

MURDER AT
PIRATE'S COVE

SECRETS & SCRABBLE BOOK ONE

JOSH LANYON

VELLICHOR BOOKS

An imprint of JustJoshin Publishing, Inc.

MURDER AT PIRATE'S COVE: AN M/M COZY MYSTERY
(Secrets and Scrabble Book 1)
February 2020
Copyright (c) 2020 by Josh Lanyon
Edited by Keren Reed
All rights reserved

Published in the United States of America

JustJoshin Publishing, Inc.
3053 Rancho Vista Blvd.
Suite 116
Palmdale, CA 93551
www.joshlanyon.com

This is a work of fiction. Any resemblance to persons living or dead is entirely coincidental.

This is dedicated to my dear friend and mod Carlita, who, frankly, embodies the word Dedication.

Time with so much truth to kill
Leaves you by the window sill so tied
Without a wing, to take you high
Without a clue to tell you why

"Rolling Home"Eric Andersen

PROLOGUE

The damp night air was bracingly cold and, as always, suffused with the distinct ocean smell. Supposedly that seaside scent came from bacteria digesting dead phytoplankton. Ellery had picked that tidbit up that afternoon from a Tripp Ellis thriller.

The streets were quiet and strangely deserted as he walked back from the pub to the bookstore. His car—well, Great-great-great-aunt Eudora's car, if someone wanted to get technical—was still in the parking lot. Captain's Seat, Great-great-great-aunt Eudora's decrepit mansion, was about a fifteen-minute drive from the village. Walking distance for someone who hadn't been on his feet all day and didn't mind a stroll down a pitch-black country road. None of which described Ellery.

His thoughts were preoccupied as he turned the corner onto the narrow brick street that held the little bookshop that had brought him to Pirate's Cove in the first place.

The tall Victorian buildings cast deep shadows. Most of the storefronts were dark or illuminated only by the faint glow of emergency lights, so he was startled to see the bright yellow oblongs stretching from the tall windows of the Crow's Nest across the gray pavement.

That's weird.

He was positive he had locked the place up after shutting all the lights off. A larger than usual electricity bill was the last thing he wanted.

He sped up, his footsteps echoing down the silent street as he hurried toward the Crow's Nest. He grabbed the doorknob, guiltily recalling that the first words Chief Carson had ever spoken to him concerned replacing the sticky old lock with a new deadbolt. His dismay ratcheted up another notch as the door swung open on well-oiled hinges.

Oh no.

No way had he forgotten to lock up. He had lived in New York most of his life, for heaven's sake. Locking doors was second nature to him. Sure, Pirate's Cove was a small town, but all you had to do was flip through a couple of titles in the cozy-mystery section to know that evil lurked in the cutest, quaintest corners of the universe.

"Hello?" he called.

His uneasy gaze fell on the thing lying just a few feet inside the shop. A purple-plumed tricorn hat. He looked past the hat, and his breath caught. His heart shuddered to a stop.

"No," he whispered. "No way…"

At first glance there appeared to be a drunken pirate passed out on the floor of the Crow's Nest. His disbelieving eyes took in the glossy boots, black velvet breeches, long, plum-colored coat and gold-trimmed vest, the scarlet lace jabot…

Scarlet.

Because the lacy folds were soaked in blood. The same blood slowly spreading around the motionless—terrifyingly motionless—form sprawled on newly sanded hardwood floors.

He put a hand out to steady himself—except there was nothing to grab—so he stumbled forward, landing on his knees beside the body. He instinctively reached to check for... But there was no need. The eerie stillness of the man's chest, the glassy stare, the gray and bloodless face... Trevor Maples was dead. Tiny, twin, horror-stricken reflections of himself in those sightless blue eyes.

He drew back, climbed clumsily to his feet, and staggered out the open door to the uncannily silent street.

"Help!" he cried. "Help! Murder!"

One by one, the street's lamps turned on as residents in the apartments above the shops surrounding the Crow's Nest woke to the cries of death and disaster. The windows of normally sleepy little Pirate's Cove lit up like the stars winking overhead.

CHAPTER ONE

A few hours earlier...

Ellery Page was thinking of murder.

Given that he was standing in the middle of a mystery bookstore, maybe that wasn't surprising.

Or maybe it was, since he had never expected to be the owner of a bookstore, mystery or otherwise. However, Ellery was not thinking of fictional murders. He was not thinking of locked-room or impossible mysteries, nor romantic suspense (definitely *not* romantic anything) nor serial-killer thrillers. Nope. He was thinking of picking up the small bronze crow (it was actually a raven, had Great-great-great-aunt Eudora only known) paperweight and conking Trevor Maples over the head.

"Yes or no?" Trevor demanded, oblivious to the tension hanging in the air of the Crow's Nest bookshop. It was the middle of the day, and the sunlight off the ocean filtered through the big bay windows of the corner shop, glancing off the row of ships' lanterns lining the back wall. The light reflecting off the glass, prismed in sea glass flashes of blue and green, created the charming illusion of an undersea grotto.

Well, it wasn't all illusion. Financially speaking, the shop was definitely underwater.

Which was why it made sense to accept Trevor's offer.

"Same answer as before," Ellery replied. "No."

No one had ever accused him of being overly sensible.

"I don't understand you," Trevor protested. "You asked for more money. I've upped my original offer *twice*."

"I *didn't* ask for more money. *You* said I was holding out for more money and that you wouldn't raise your offer."

Trevor's buffed, professionally manicured nails beat impatiently against the wooden counter. *Tap, tap, tap. Tap, tap, tap.* Each time his fingertips hit the counter, Ellery tried not to wince. Trevor was, at least in his own opinion, kind of a big deal in Pirate's Cove. He owned three of the most successful shops in the village and was currently the leading candidate for mayor.

Apparently, the fact that the Crow's Nest had a few dusty first editions for sale put Ellery in direct competition with Gimcrack Antiques, Trevor's most successful business enterprise, but Ellery found that hard to believe. The Crow's Nest had been foundering for a long time. He had to believe there was some other more pressing reason that Trevor was so determined to buy him out. So determined, in fact, that he'd shown up on a Saturday morning, taking time out from his campaigning. This made it his third attempt in as many weeks to buy the Crow's Nest.

"You said the shop held no sentimental value for you. You never even met Eudora. What else *could* you mean besides wanting more money?"

Trevor looked around at the store as he waited for Ellery's answer. His lip curled.

It wasn't hard to read his mind. Great-great-great-aunt Eudora had died in February, and though Ellery had been working steadily for the last three months, trying to get everything shipshape, you couldn't undo forty years of dust and disorganization just like that. To add to the challenge, Great-great-great-aunt Eudora had been quite a hoarder during the last few years of her life. Every time Ellery had to go down to the cellar, he feared he would be crushed beneath one of those teetering towers of moldy paperbacks.

"Well?" Trevor cocked a gingery eyebrow at Ellery. He looked pointedly at his open checkbook.

"Well what?"

"What is it you want, if not money?" *Tap, tap, tap.* Trevor's fingers drummed across the wood a little faster as his impatience grew.

"It's not about money," Ellery said.

Trevor drawled, "It's *always* about money."

And he wasn't completely wrong. The offer of a ready-made home and business had definitely factored into Ellery's decision to leave his life in New York. Timing had also been a consideration. Opportunity had knocked in the form of Great-great-great-aunt Eudora's passing, and Ellery had answered.

Someone behind the tall shelf of espionage and spy thrillers coughed. Ellery hadn't realized there were any customers in the shop. That was a good sign!

"So?" Trevor snapped. "What's it going to be?"

Ellery didn't want to get all expansive with Trevor, but he needed these impromptu visits to stop, and maybe he hadn't been clear enough in their previous conversations. He said, a little apologetically because he did not like confrontation, "The thing is, Mr. Maples, my inheriting this bookstore gave me a chance to start over. I was ready to start fresh, and this is the opportunity I was waiting for. I like Pirate's Cove. I'm getting to love living in a small town. I even sort of enjoy running a bookstore—"

"You don't have to leave Pirate's Cove," Trevor interrupted. "I'm not running you out of town. You can stay in the village. You can even stay on in the bookstore, working for me. I can always use good help, and you've done an impre—

decent job of cleaning out this rat's nest and getting the shop up and running."

What an ass.

Ellery said firmly, "I'm sorry, the Crow's Nest is not for sale." His cheeks hurt with the effort of keeping his pleasant smile *up and running*.

Trevor looked as taken aback as if the bronze paperweight had spoken up. His expression hardened. "I see," he said dryly. "Fine. Name your price. I'll pay whatever you want. Within reason, of course."

Did Trevor really think this was all about negotiating for a better deal? Yeah, he probably did, because that was what he would be doing in Ellery's place. Anyway, what the heck was his obsession with taking over the Crow's Nest? Pirate's Cove was surely large enough to support two antiques shops or two bookstores or two anythings. Especially in the summer, when business picked up. That was the rumor, at least. Business picked up when the weather turned warm and the tourists arrived.

Of course, if Trevor's claim that Great-great-great-aunt Eudora had promised to sell to him was true, his frustration with the way things had turned out was understandable. But according to Mr. Landry, Great-great-great-aunt Eudora's lawyer, no such sale had been in the works. In fact, Mr. Landry insisted Great-great-great-aunt Eudora would never have willingly sold to Trevor.

Maybe it would have been different if Trevor wasn't so arrogant, so pushy. His offer was a fair one—and this new offer was likely more than fair—and it was true that Ellery had no sentimental attachment to the shop or to the bookselling business. With the money from the sale of the Crow's Nest he could open another business, maybe even one with a better chance of success. But Trevor was so unpleasant, it made even someone as easygoing as Ellery want to thwart him.

"That's very generous, but no."

Trevor glowered. "Yes, it *is* generous. And it's a limited-time offer."

Ellery shrugged.

"You can't be serious." Trevor's voice rose. "This place is practically falling down around your ears. You don't know the first thing about running a bookstore. And for all your talk about second chances and loving life in a small town, we both know you're not going to stick around for long. You don't belong here."

Wow. Really? Trevor was one step from telling him, *We don't take kindly to your sort around these parts!*

Maybe he was right. Maybe it was true. But as much as Ellery didn't like confrontation, he had a stubborn streak, and the more Trevor insisted he *had* to sell, the more certain Ellery became that no way was he selling to Trevor.

"Sorry. I really don't know what else to tell you. The Crow's Nest is not for sale. Not now. Not ever." *Not to you.* Ellery managed not to say that last aloud, but it was probably in his tone.

Trevor stared at him for a long moment. "We'll see," he said finally. He even smiled. It was not a nice smile. "I'll give you twenty-four hours to change your mind. I suggest you think long and hard about the future. Especially if you're planning on spending it in *my* town."

The threat was hard to miss. Ellery said nothing. He was thinking Trevor was like the villain in a bad movie—maybe a Hallmark movie because there was no physical threat and even the nonphysical threat was vague. Clearly Trevor believed he had the election in the bag.

Snidely Whiplash, a.k.a. Trevor, knew better than to waste a good exit line. He turned and headed for the front entrance. The bell tinkled cheerily as he opened the door, and then again as the door banged shut. The antique cutlass hanging above the frame slipped off one of its hooks, and the blade swung down, slicing through the air in a deadly arc.

CHAPTER TWO

Ellery stared at the dangling sword and gulped.

Talk about a lawsuit waiting to happen.

He left the counter and went to find a hammer and nails, sparing a glance behind the rows of bookshelves. The customer of earlier was gone now, no doubt slipping out unnoticed as Ellery and Trevor's argument had grown more heated.

Ellery located a hammer in the office desk drawer, but no nails. He dragged the stool behind the counter out, climbed up to study the hooks over the door. One had nearly worked its way out. Ellery gave it a couple of solid bangs, rehung the cutlass, and jumped down from the stool.

The rusty blade of the sword was a reminder of how much work still needed to be done in the shop. Never mind the big barn of a house he had inherited along with the business. At least Great-great-great-aunt Eudora had made an effort—however unsuccessful—to maintain order at the Crow's Nest. The house, a smallish Victorian mansion a few miles outside the village, was literally falling down. In fact, the night before last, a window in the master bedroom had slid right out of its frame and smashed to pieces in the overgrown jungle that had once been the rose garden.

Maybe he *should* consider Trevor's offer. There was no guarantee he could turn the business around, and if he failed, what then? He'd have squandered this windfall on a pipedream. His friends back home in New York all thought he was crazy to take this on—and had had no hesitation in telling him so. And there was no question he missed his old life. He missed his friends, he missed the theater, the city, he even occasionally missed Todd.

Well, maybe not Todd himself, but no question Todd's absence left a hole in his life. It had been nice at the end of the day to have someone to share all the ups and downs with, even if he'd spent the other ninety percent of the time arguing with that same someone. He didn't miss the arguing, that was for sure.

Anyway, if he abandoned ship now, he would feel like a failure. A *real* failure. Because there was a big difference between not succeeding and just giving up. He *needed* this change. He needed a fresh start. As much as he loved New York, the city had become a giant dead end for him. Whereas Pirate's Cove, small as it was, contained endless possibilities.

Ellery gazed around at the towering wooden bookshelves and sea-themed oil paintings lining the walls, and felt a flicker of satisfaction. He'd spent a lot of time painting walls, washing windows, sanding floors, and polishing furniture, and if you didn't peer too closely at all the wear and tear from years of damp ocean air, the Crow's Nest looked cozy and quaint.

All he really needed now was for the store to sell enough to keep it afloat.

And so far…yikes.

Ellery returned the hammer to the drawer in the office desk, pausing to consider a stack of Riker display cases filled with shells, seahorses, and starfish. He'd removed most of the grimy paintings, tattered posters, and total junk cluttering the walls in order to repaint. He'd rehung the best of the paintings but left the white walls otherwise clean and bare, giving the shop a more open, airy feel. But these display boxes were pretty cool. Maybe if he hung them at the ends of the dark shelves?

He heard the front entrance bell jingle, and tensed. Not again. He'd *thought* Trevor gave up too easily that time.

Ellery charged out of the office, fully prepared for round two, so it was a surprise to find a tall, dark-haired woman dressed in complete pirate wench costume, standing on the other side of the counter.

"Ahoy there, matey," she drawled in a deep, slightly sexy voice.

Uh…right. Because today was the official start of Buccaneer Days, a weeklong celebration of Pirate's Cove's murky and probably nefarious history. Ostensibly, Buccaneer Days had been conceived as a way of attracting tourists off-season to this windswept southern coast of Rhode Island, but having worked in theater for most of his adult life, Ellery knew people loved any excuse to play dress-up.

"Hi. Can I help you?"

"Maybe we can help each other. I'm Tommy Rider." She flashed Ellery a beguiling smile, offering her hand.

It took him a moment, but then he remembered that Thomasina Rider was the main real-estate agent for Pirate's Cove. They'd never formally met, though they'd had some email correspondence regarding the deed to Great-great-great-aunt Eudora's house.

"Right. Nice to meet you at last."

They shook hands, and Ellery did his best to avoid staring down into Tommy's gold-embroidered green-velvet bustier. His preference ran on different lines, but no question she was quite striking. He guessed she had probably done some modeling.

"If I'd realized what I was missing, I'd have hightailed it over here sooner. Are you sure you're a screenwriter and not an actor?"

Ellery smiled. He didn't take her flattery seriously. For one thing, it was obvious her default setting was *flirtatious*. For another, he was well aware of his looks. When he'd been younger, he'd been very self-conscious, but at thirty-two he had learned to accept that through some fluke of biology, he'd hit the genetic jackpot. His wavy hair was dark brown, his wide eyes hazel, his bone structure elegantly masculine. He was six feet tall and lightly muscled—okay, the muscles were not inherited; he took pains to stay fit because writing was not exactly a physically demanding job.

"That was the first plan," he admitted. "It turns out I can't act my way out of a paper bag."

Tommy chuckled. "No? Well, TV's loss is our gain. Anyway, I decided it was time to finally meet you in person and see how the Crow's Nest is coming along." She glanced around the shop. "Good God. I have to say, you've worked wonders here. I've never seen the place look so clean and bright and inviting. No wonder Trevor's hounding you to sell to him."

Ellery grimaced. "I didn't realize that was common knowledge."

"Oh, sugar, *everything* is common knowledge in a village." Tommy's gaze wandered around the shop once more. "Yes, this is pretty impressive. Poor old Eudora would be thrilled." Her bright gaze returned to Ellery's. "What's your asking price?"

"I don't have one. I'm not interested in selling."

She nodded thoughtfully.

An unpleasant suspicion dawned. "Are you here on Trevor's behalf?"

Tommy gave another of those husky chuckles. "No way. But if you do change your mind, I'd love to handle the property for you."

"You're the most popular real-estate agent in town, so if I do change my mind, you've got the commission."

They smiled at each other with perfect understanding.

"Actually, I'm here to win your vote," Tommy said. "As you may or may not know, I'm running for mayor against Trevor in the upcoming election."

"I saw that."

"As of this morning, I'm in second place."

Cyrus Jones, Pirate Cove's current mayor, was bringing up the rear in the three-way race for mayor. It was surprising how hotly contested the election was, given that fewer than four thousand citizens inhabited the entire island.

"Congratulations," Ellery said.

"Well, it's too soon for congratulations, which is why I would really appreciate *your* vote." Tommy took a moment to flutter her lash extensions in his direction. "Here's a pamphlet you can take home to read. It describes the platforms I'm running on and the promises I intend to keep for the citizens of Pirate's Cove."

"Okay," Ellery said doubtfully. He didn't have a spare moment to read things he might actually enjoy, let alone what likely amounted to a glossy, full-color sales pitch.

"I look forward to earning your vote!" One scarlet-tipped fingernail slid across the scratched counter an ocean-blue pamphlet featuring Tommy's beaming smile. The living, breathing Tommy winked at him.

"Thanks. You're in my top three contenders." He accepted the pamphlet, giving it a quick, curious glance. As he'd suspected, it seemed to be mostly advertising for Rider Realty.

Tommy chuckled. She had a surprisingly deep and un-expectedly appealing laugh. "That's a start." She was already making her way back to the door.

"Lovely to meet you, Ellery. I'm sure we'll run into each other again. Oh, and don't worry too much about Trevor; he's more bark than bite." The familiar bell tinkled through the salty morning air, and the door closed, cutting off Tommy's voice. Ellery was smiling faintly as he returned to studying her brochure.

CHAPTER THREE

Bookish buccaneers did not appear to be a thing.

That Saturday Ellery sold a mass-market paperback of Agatha Christie's *The Hollow*, a paperback edition of Robert Crais's *The Monkey's Raincoat*, and three fabric-covered, tasseled bookmarks for a day's grand total of thirty-five dollars and twenty-two cents. The afternoon turned into evening, and he couldn't help wondering if he had been too hasty in declining Trevor's offer.

At six thirty, he closed up shop and headed over to the Salty Dog for dinner. He wasn't quite ready to brave the Miss Havisham vibe and depressingly empty fridge of Captain's Seat. He wanted a drink and a nice meal—and an hour or so of efficient central heating.

Libby Tulley, the teenaged daughter of Tom Tulley, owner and proprietor of the pub, led Ellery to his usual spot: a quiet corner table positioned between the cozy stone fireplace and the window overlooking Main Street. This vantage point allowed Ellery, a devoted people-watcher, to indulge his voyeuristic tendencies without putting him center stage for the viewing pleasure of his neighbors.

His neighbors for now, because after today's dismal sales, he wasn't sure how much longer he could support the shop before they both went bankrupt. He had already gone through the little money left to him by Great-great-great-aunt

Eudora in order to renovate the Crow's Nest. He was living off his own savings, which had seemed like plenty when he'd arrived three months ago, but which were dwindling fast. He simply did not have the financial resources to begin repairs on the old mansion, keep the bookstore afloat, and put food in his belly.

Ellery sighed. He considered himself a reasonably optimistic and resilient person, but maybe he should have stayed in the Big Apple.

Where he belonged?

Yeah, maybe. Maybe Trevor had been right about that. Studying the noisy and crowded pub, where everyone but himself appeared to be clad in full swashbuckler regalia, he couldn't help feeling like a fish out of water.

Before he could get too downhearted, Libby, pert and ginger-haired, appeared with a frosty mug of "grog," and recited the evening specials: shepherd's pie, meatloaf dinner, and baked mac-and-cheese casserole. In other words, the same specials as every other night. Ellery gave in to the call of carbs and opted for the mac and cheese.

The blend of soft lights, grog (rum—a lot of rum—lime, sugar, and beer) and the jolly soundtrack to *Pirates of the Caribbean* gradually eased his tension.

He could probably hold out for another two months, and by then it would be tourist season and perhaps business would pick up. It could hardly get worse.

His dismal reflections were interrupted by Libby, who finally placed his mac-and-cheese casserole on the table before him.

"*Bon appétit!*" Libby said.

"*Merci,*" Ellery replied.

Libby snickered as though this were a great witticism, and he grinned. Over her shoulder he spied Police Chief Jack

Carson being led to *his* regular table on the opposite side of the pub, and he felt an instant and unwilling leap of interest.

Partly that was because Carson was a ruggedly handsome six foot, one hundred and ninety-plus pounds of gainfully employed eligible male. He wore a wedding ring—he might even *be* married—but from the moment Ellery's gaze had first tangled with the police chief's piercing green-blue one, he had been pretty sure Carson had a secret that would deeply disappoint the ladies of Pirate's Cove. That was speculation on Ellery's part. He certainly had nothing more than a certain gut instinct—his interactions with the chief had been minimal at most—but yeah. He couldn't help hoping he was right. Not because he had a personal interest in Carson—after Todd, he was through with all that—but because as far as Ellery could tell, he was the only LGBTQ person on all of Buck Island. It would be nice to have some company, even if the company was not of the socializing variety. Initially, he'd thought Dylan Carter, who owned the toy shop next door to the Crow's Nest, was of the same orientation, but it turned out Dylan was just a flamboyant guy with a slightly effeminate manner. Which was a good lesson about judging people based on appearances.

Anyway, Carson was in his late thirties, had sun-streaked brown hair and eyes the changeful color of sunlight on restless water. His voice was surprisingly pleasant for a guy who never smiled and seemed to live for handing out construction-code violations.

Ellery watched the chief—clad in his usual navy uniform and not pirate garb—nodding politely to the local wives and wenches bidding him good evening. He picked up his menu, putting an end to the pleasantries. That had to be deliberate, because as often as the chief ate at the Salty Dog, he surely knew the entire menu by heart. Ellery did, and he'd only been in Pirate's Cove three months.

Ellery gave the Ritz-cracker crust of his mac and cheese a tentative poke. Frankly, the casserole could have been topped with Oreos for all he cared. He was too hungry to be picky. He couldn't afford to hire any help at the bookstore, so lunch usually consisted of whatever he could eat at the front desk. Today's fare had been a bag of granola and a Kona Blend Monster Energy drink.

The door to the pub opened on a blustery gust of salt-laced night air. A group of pirates carrying guitar and mandolin cases pushed their way through the crowd, which greeted them with song requests and offers to buy drinks. The piped-in music cut off mid-ballad.

My heart, my heart, my drowning heart...

Ellery glanced over at Chief Carson's table and found the chief studying him with his usual unsmiling appraisal. His face warmed, his heart jumped—that was guilty conscience over the fact that he still hadn't fixed the ceiling vents in the customers' bathroom—and he nodded politely.

Carson nodded grimly back and returned to frowning over the menu.

Yep, that was one steely jawline Carson sported. Smoke-detector violations were probably a hanging offense in his book.

Ellery picked up his fork. His gaze wandered again to the mostly empty street outside the pub. A couple of pickup trucks tooled past in the glimmery lamplight, and occasionally, he caught a glimpse of a bustling petticoat or a plumed hat disappearing around a corner. But for the most part, everyone in Pirate's Cove seemed to be crammed inside the Salty Dog.

Happily, that did not include Trevor Maples, though he was usually present most evenings. In fact, the last time he'd been there, he'd once again tried to convince Ellery to sell him the Crow's Nest. *No* did not seem to be in Trevor's vocabulary.

Ellery swallowed the last mouthful of grog, finished his casserole, paid his bill, and rose to leave.

By then the band—the Fish and Chippies—had broken into a lively version of "Eddystone Light."

He glanced automatically toward Chief Carson's corner and, aggravatingly, Carson, engaged in conversation with Tom Tulley, seemed to feel the weight of his gaze and glanced over at him.

Hastily, Ellery shrugged into his jacket and headed for the door.

CHAPTER FOUR

A few hours later...

"I don't know how he got inside or what he was doing in the bookshop."

Ellery was seated in his back office, trying to cover up the fact that he was completely and totally freaked out by recent events. Not that being freaked out wasn't a normal reaction, but something about Police Chief Carson brought out a previously undiscovered need to appear cool in a crisis. Frankly, he was not really a cool-in-a-crisis kind of guy. He was the kind of guy who yelled, *"Help! Murder!"* when he found a body.

"How did you know Maples had been murdered?" had been one of Chief Carson's first questions.

"Possibly the pool of blood was a clue?" Ellery had snapped.

"Maybe he committed suicide. Maybe he tripped over the doorstop I asked you to remove two weeks ago."

Ellery managed to swallow his retort.

So yeah, he was that kind of guy. The kind who got sarcastic when put on the defensive, the kind who felt queasy and a little light-headed in the presence of dead bodies and had to be told by Chief Carson not to faint or throw up on the crime scene.

Speaking of which—or whom—Ellery was quickly getting over his slight and very brief interest in Chief Carson. Chief Carson had turned out to be an insensitive, unimaginative jerk.

Anyway. It had been hours since Ellery had first crept into the Crow's Nest and found Trevor Maples, clad in pirate costume, dead on his floor. Chief Carson had been first on the scene, but to Ellery's relief, the chief was not the only law-enforcement officer in Pirate's Cove. He actually had several trained officers in his teeny-tiny police department and access to the full resources of the Rhode Island State Police. In fact, Ellery had assumed the State Police would take over the investigation, but no. It seemed that at least for now, Chief Carson was still in charge.

And covering the same ground over and over. For example, this was the second time they'd been over the subject of how and why Trevor had decided to turn up dead in Ellery's bookshop. What else was there to say beyond *I. Don't. Know*?

Of course, murder had to be a new experience for the chief too. The nearest thing to crime Pirate's Cove experienced was a bit of drunk and disorderly on the weekends. Maybe Carson was also feeling defensive. Maybe he was worried the State Police were going to take away his first and only murder case.

"When was the last time you spoke to Maples?" Carson asked. This too was not a new question. Did he think if he changed his wording, he might get a different answer?

"I told you," Ellery replied. "This afternoon. He offered to buy the Crow's Nest again. He told me I could name my price—within reason."

Were Carson's eyes more green than blue? It was hard to tell. The only thing for sure was they were as bright and hard as sea glass. "And what was your price?"

"I told him I didn't want to sell."

The dark and forbidding line of Carson's brows rose skeptically. "And did he buy that?"

Ellery was momentarily confused. "Did he—"

Carson said with a trace of impatience, "Did he *accept* your refusal?"

"Oh. No. I don't know. I think he thought I was still negotiating for a better price."

"Were you?"

"No."

"*No?*" Carson didn't bother trying to hide his disbelief.

Ellery shook his head. "I like it here. I told him that. I wouldn't be going to all this trouble of renovating the shop if my plan was just to sell."

Carson looked taken aback. Or at least as taken aback as someone like him could look. "You're planning to stay in Pirate's Cove?"

"Well, yes. That was the idea. That was my great-aunt's idea."

Brow furrowed, Carson jotted down a couple of notes in a small black book. He had long fingers. His hands were tanned and strong, but the nails were neatly trimmed and filed. He wore a plain-gold wedding band on his left hand. Not exactly conclusive proof, but... The scratching of his pencil was the only sound filling the void of silence stretching between them.

Ellery watched uneasily. His mind was racing. Carson couldn't think he'd done it. Could he? That was preposterous. And yet, there was something going on here, something in Carson's attitude that made Ellery nervous. What was it that Carson knew and Ellery didn't?

"How's the shop doing?" Carson asked without looking up from his notes.

Ellery shrugged.

Carson raised his head. "Could you be more specific?"

"From what everyone tells me, this is the slow season."

Carson's mouth curved without humor. "But you're turning a profit?"

"No."

"You're breaking even?"

Ellery grimaced. "No."

"You're losing money." It was not a question.

Why was Carson hammering away on this point? Ellery said cautiously, "The renovations cost money, but that's to be expected."

Carson pushed back in his chair, said almost conversationally, "I remember your aunt. She was quite a character. And not one to beat about the bush. According to her, the Crow's Nest had been running in the red for some time. The last time I spoke to her, she was weighing whether to sell up or close the doors for good."

Ellery's sinking confidence sprang another leak.

"Was she going to sell to Trevor Maples?"

"You tell me."

Ellery stared into Chief Carson's eyes. He could see Carson wanted to get his reaction, so okay. His reaction was confusion and guilt. If Great-great-great-aunt Eudora really had agreed to sell to Trevor, Trevor's persistence made more sense.

"All I know is my great-aunt left the bookstore and her house to me, and I'm doing my best to turn things around. The business is doing as expected for this time of year. If there was an agreement with Trevor, I'm unaware of it. And Mr. Landry, Great-great-great-aunt Eudora's lawyer, was unaware of it."

Chief Carson nodded, made another note. "How would you describe your relationship with Mr. Maples?"

Trevor had been telling the truth the whole time. No wonder he had been so impatient and exasperated with Ellery's decision to stay in Pirate's Cove. Especially when it was probably obvious that Ellery had no more chance of making the Crow's Nest a success than Great-great-great-aunt Eudora had.

"Mr. Page?" Chief Carson's voice broke through Ellery's reverie. He stared at the chief. Carson was tall and lean. He had an athletic build, but he didn't tower, he wasn't physically imposing. So why did it feel like he was taking up all the space in the small office?

"What?"

"Tell me about your relationship with Mr. Maples."

"There was no relationship. He wanted to buy the bookstore. I didn't want to sell. He wasn't used to being told no." Ellery shrugged.

"It's fair to say the relationship was contentious?"

"I don't know that it's fair to say that. It's not like we exchanged words." Actually, yes, today's encounter probably qualified as exchanging words. Both he and Trevor had been testy, and toward the end, Trevor had bordered on threatening. Ellery revised, "It's not like we came to blows."

"How many times would you say you and Maples argued?"

Meeting Carson's cool and steady gaze, Ellery felt his scalp prickle with unease. "I'm not sure where you're going with this, Chief, but you saw me in the Salty Dog this evening. I have an alibi. *You* can confirm my alibi. Right?"

"I saw you in the Salty Dog just after seven this evening. You were there for about forty-five minutes," Carson agreed. "The ME's preliminary examination puts Maples's time of death between five and seven p.m. So as alibis go…"

Ellery could think of nothing to say. Should he keep quiet? Should he keep trying to explain? What was the real-life protocol? He had nothing to hide, and yet it was increasingly clear that Carson believed he was somehow involved.

Did Carson believe that? Or were these just basic interrogation tactics? It felt like they'd been sitting here covering the same ground for a very long time, but maybe that was how it was supposed to work.

Carson said briskly, "Mr. Page, if I may ask, where were you tonight between five p.m. and seven p.m.?"

"Here. In the Crow's Nest. The shop was still open at five o'clock. I didn't close up until six thirty."

"Can anyone confirm that? Did you have customers? Deliveries? Did anyone stop by to chat?"

"I…"

No. His last sale had been at three that afternoon. He had received no deliveries that day. After the sale of the bookmarks, he did not recall anyone walking into the shop even to use the restroom.

Ellery had never been a fan of crime shows or mystery novels, but three months of running a mystery bookstore had given him a rudimentary understanding of how murder investigations worked. At least in fiction.

He said, "Wouldn't someone have heard the shot?"

The downcast black crescents of Carson's eyelashes flicked up. He studied Ellery. "Shot?"

"Yes. The businesses on either side of me stay open until five. If Trevor had walked into the Crow's Nest and I'd shot him, surely someone would have heard that?"

After a moment, Carson said, "Maybe you used a silencer."

"Where would I get a silencer? I'm not a hitman. I don't even own a gun, let alone a silencer."

There was something odd about Carson's expression. Ellery's theater experience meant he was pretty good at reading facial expressions, but he couldn't interpret that particular blankness on Carson's face.

"What you're saying is, no one can corroborate your claim that the shop was still open until six thirty."

"I'm not saying that. I'm saying I can't think of anyone. But someone could have noticed. One of my neighbors or maybe someone walking past."

Ellery wasn't sure if he was more scared or more exasperated. How could Carson think he had anything to do with this? Did he have *no* instinct for people?

"This is such a ridiculous scenario. You're suggesting I killed someone and then calmly went to dinner and then came back here and pretended to find the body?"

"It's not as far-fetched as you might imagine."

Oh brother. And Carson had gleaned this from all his years of policing the mean streets of Pirate's Cove?

"The forensics people checked my hands. Wouldn't they have seen the gunpowder residue or whatever you call it?"

Carson was giving him that odd look again. He said finally—almost growled it, really, "It doesn't work like that."

"Well, how does it work?"

"*I'll* ask the questions."

"I don't think *that's* very fair!" Ellery protested. "When I might be able to come up with something that helps my case?"

Carson scribbled into his notebook, muttered, "Pretty unlikely."

"No, it's not. What's my motive? Tell me that?"

He kind of wished he hadn't asked because Carson's expression grew more closed, his eyes turning as bleak and chilly as the winter shoreline.

"I'd say your motive for getting rid of Maples is the same as his for wanting to buy you out. You're both struggling to survive in a town that can't support one of you, let alone both."

It was *almost* funny.

"You think I killed Trevor to wipe out my competition?"

"Did you?"

"No! That's..." The words dried in Ellery's throat at the expression in Chief Carson's fierce eyes. "*No.*"

"But you admit Maples was your main competition?"

He was serious. Ellery's eyes widened in alarm. "No. Trevor sells books, but they're all antiques, first editions and that kind of thing. He considered himself an antiquarian. I'm not—I'm just a guy running an ordinary bookstore."

The chief said nothing.

"Besides, most of Trevor's business was antique furniture. We weren't really competitors."

"According to Maples, you were."

It was Ellery's turn to keep silent. He was pretty sure he already said way too much.

One of Carson's deputies stuck his head in the office. "We're wrapping things up now, Chief."

Carson nodded. "Thanks, Martin."

Ellery pushed to his feet, ignoring the wobble in his knees. "Is that it? Or am I under arrest?"

A lifetime seemed to pass waiting for Carson's reply. When it came, it was almost disconcertingly prosaic.

"That's it for now." Carson laid his pencil on his open notebook. "Thanks for your cooperation. You can go."

"Aren't you going to tell me not to leave town?"

"Are you planning to leave town? Fifteen minutes ago, you told me you planned to stay in Pirate's Cove."

"I am. Planning to stay, I mean."

"Good. This is an ongoing investigation. The expectation is you'll keep yourself available for further questioning."

Ellery swallowed. He suspected it looked and sounded like a gulp.

Carson nodded at the door in dismissal. Ellery headed out of the office, his knees nearly giving out as Carson said, "One other thing."

Ellery turned, unspeaking.

"I'll need you to inventory the store and let me know what, if anything, is missing."

Ellery nodded.

"And I'll need that as soon as possible."

"Yes. Of course," Ellery got out.

Carson nodded again, and turned back to his notes.

The medical examiner had already come and gone, collecting Trevor's body for the morgue and subsequent autopsy. Ellery's queasiness returned at the thought.

He couldn't help feeling that the uniformed officers and crime-scene investigators were staring at him accusingly as he quickly gathered his coat and other belongings, heading for the front door.

Maybe he would sell the shop.

He was pretty sure he would never be able to think of it the same way. Never look at the place where Trevor's body had lain without forever seeing that ghastly, bloodstained image. He risked a quick look, expecting to see a chalk outline, but his uneasy peek revealed nothing more than a couple of plastic markers and a pool of stomach-churning crimson staining the floorboards.

Here was a problem. Who would he sell the shop to, now that Trevor was gone?

One of PCPD's finest began to turn off the lights, row after row of bell-shaped lamps going black.

Another uniformed officer pushed open the front door for Ellery. The little bell tinkled with almost sinister good cheer, the sound cutting off as the door swung shut behind him with a curt *bang*.

CHAPTER FIVE

Sunday morning found Ellery prying loose cracked and peeling moss-colored linoleum from his kitchen floor—and trying to wipe the image of Trevor Maples's sightless eyes from his memory.

There was always a chance the 18th Century architect of Captain's Seat had not been on crack when he drew up the plans for the sprawling Dutch Renaissance style mansion. But how likely was that?

In Ellery's opinion, not very.

But then again, maybe it wasn't the architect's fault. Maybe the skewed artistic vision had belonged to the original owner, Captain Horatio Page. Back in the 1700s, Page had been a famed hunter of pirates, eventually retiring to this quiet little corner of Rhode Island. Maybe he had liked remembering his glory days. Maybe he just had a taste for architectural bling.

In fairness, a couple of centuries ago, the house had probably been a bit of a showstopper with its distinctive curved gables, stained-glass windows, and twin conical-shaped rooftops. The exterior was made of slate-colored locally quarried granite. The interior was paneled in white oak, the lower level windows were arched segmental ones like on a pirate galleon, the mismatched flooring reportedly came from the timbers of ships crashed to pieces on the jagged coastline.

Quaint, yes. Cozy... Captain's Seat had six bedrooms and seven baths. The bedrooms were large. Large enough for every single one to have its own fireplace. Along with all the bedrooms came a grand foyer, a great hall, a gallery, a drawing room, a library, a game room—that had been a thrill to the former reigning Scrabble champion of the Manhattan Scrabble Meetup Group—a pantry and a wine cellar. No doubt it had required a fleet of servants to keep everything shipshape and Bristol back in the day.

Nowadays...

Even if extreme housekeeping had been in Ellery's wheelhouse, the place was falling down around his ears. Literally around his ears. Two nights earlier an ornate lantern-shaped sconce had fallen off his bedroom wall and nearly knocked him out while he stood brushing his teeth in front of the life-sized portrait of his distant ancestor.

The mansion was full of charming, murderous decor. Like the chipped and peeling mermaid figurehead dangling over the mile-long dining-room table, or the banisters built to look like the row of cannons on the broadside of a warship, or the gigantic bronze shell that had once decorated the stern of a French frigate but now hung over the fireplace in the "great hall."

The roof leaked, windowpanes fell like rotting teeth, and some of the floorboards were see-through. The entire place smelled of must, dust, and rust.

Okay, so maybe it wasn't that bad. Or rather, it was that bad, but it was also undeniably the coolest house he'd ever been in. There was *a trapdoor* in his bedroom, for heaven's sake! It just didn't get better than that. If he'd had unlimited time and a couple of extra million dollars, there was nothing Ellery would have enjoyed more than restoring Captain's Seat to its original manic glory. As it was, he had one day a week—Sunday—a cordless drill, and his trusty hammer.

He was not making a lot of headway, although he had managed to get the master bedroom into reasonable shape— barring the occasional outbreak of homicidal lighting fixtures. Actually, he was pretty happy with the way his bedroom had turned out. The large corner room overlooked both the wide, overgrown meadows behind the house and the green and rocky ocean cliffs in the front. In the morning, buttery sunshine warmed the polished oak panels and brass fixtures, turning the room as gold as pirates' bounty. In the evening, he could see the stars and hear the distant crash of waves and the call of the owl that lived in the garret.

Anyway, after the horror of Saturday, it was a relief to stick close to home and hearth. Ellery tried to focus on the job at hand—removing the ghastly mid-century green vinyl tile in the kitchen—but despite his best efforts, he couldn't help brooding over the previous day's events.

The shock of being suspected of murder—and the fear of being arrested for that crime—had initially so overwhelmed him that it wasn't until Sunday morning that it occurred to him a murderer was loose in Pirate's Cove.

And the more he thought about it, the more convinced he was that murderous someone had deliberately tried to frame him.

Why else would Trevor's body have been dumped in his shop? (Or had Trevor been killed in the Crow's Nest?) Either way, *why*? What was there to gain by framing him?

And if he wasn't being framed, what was the point of all this? Had there been some pressing need to get rid of Trevor's body and Ellery's shop happened to be handy?

And why was Chief Carson so eager to pin this crime on him? Couldn't he see how obviously flimsy Ellery's supposed motivation was? Even Ellery knew the evidence against him was entirely circumstantial. Had the chief taken some kind of instantaneous dislike to him? Or was it simply Ellery's outsider status that made him the prime suspect? Because wasn't the victim's spouse or partner supposed to be the main suspect? Or was that only in movies and books?

Maybe Trevor hadn't had a spouse or partner. (In fact, all things considered, maybe that was a given.)

More to the point, how was it that no one had seen anything?

Sunset was around seven thirty, but yesterday had been the start of Buccaneer Days, so regardless of the time, someone would surely have been wandering the streets. Although, thinking back, yesterday had been pretty quiet. (If the goal of yesterday's exercise in wardrobe malfunction had been to attract tourists to Pirate's Cove, the Visitors Bureau needed to up their game.)

He used his utility knife to cut another six-inch-wide parallel strip of vinyl flooring. His hand slipped as he remembered the blood seeping into the floorboards at the Crow's Nest, and he banged his knuckles on the tile. Oh God. He was going to have to find a company that did crime-scene cleanup before he could reopen.

Ellery rose, went to the sink to run cold water over his hand, and through the window noticed a figure walking up the gravel pathway toward the front door. A woman in a blue skirt and brown jacket. He didn't recognize her.

Turning off the sink taps, he grabbed the towel on the counter and wiped his hands. He started for the front door and heard the doorbell chiming slowly, sonorously through the house.

He wasn't expecting visitors, and it was kind of a weird day for company. Maybe she was selling magazine subscriptions. Or maybe she'd been passing by and her car had a flat tire.

He reached the front door with its weathered planks and porthole, slid the metal bars, and opened it.

"Hi. Can I help you?"

"Ellery Page?"

"That's right." He had the sudden, uneasy feeling she was about to serve him with a court summons. There was something about her...

"Hi, I'm Sue Lewis."

"Right," he said blankly.

It surprised him that in a village the size of Pirate's Cove there were still so many new faces, so many people he had yet to meet. She was about his age, pretty and petite. Her blond hair was long and straight, her brown eyes and olive complexion perfectly made up in flattering nude tones, her clothes fashionable business. She smiled, offering a glimpse of very white teeth.

"Sue Lewis," she prompted. "Editor in chief for the *Scuttlebutt Weekly*. Our local paper?"

"*Oh,*" he said in a very different tone of voice.

Sue's smile widened with determination. "I can't believe we haven't met before now." She held out her hand.

Okay. He did not subscribe to the *Scuttlebutt Weekly*, but he did let them sell the paper in his shop. Ellery automatically shook hands. Sue had a very firm grip and did not immediately let go of him.

"I was hoping to ask you a few—" she began.

At the same time, Ellery said, "If you're here to ask about what happened last night—"

"You mean the murder in your bookstore of one of our most prominent citizens?" Sue was still smiling, but her eyes were a lot harder than he had initially thought. Not a woman used to taking no for an answer.

He dropped Sue's hand and stepped back. "I don't know anything about it," he said.

That seemed to amuse Sue. She said almost teasingly, "You must know *something* about it. Police Chief Carson interviewed you for over an hour last night."

Her comment landed like a brick in his belly. Apparently, it was true about no secrets in a small town. Was it now common knowledge that he was a suspect in Trevor Maples's murder? Were all his friends and neighbors—okay, all his neighbors—openly speculating about whether he'd actually killed Trevor? And did no one have any boundaries? Why was this woman on his doorstep, accosting him in his own home? On a Sunday no less. Wasn't church-going supposed to be a thing in villages?

"No. Sorry. I'm not giving any interviews to anyone." Ellery was firm. He reached for the door, started to close it— pausing in astonishment as Sue stepped forward, blocking him.

"What can you tell me about the fight you and Trevor had yesterday afternoon?"

"What fight? There was no fight."

"Come on, Ellery. I have an eyewitness who reported that you and Trevor got into a verbal altercation only hours before he was found dead in your shop."

"It wasn't like that at all."

"You have to admit the timing is pretty suspicious." Sue leaned in closer, and he realized she was holding a cell phone. Was she *recording* him?

"Would you move please? I'm trying to close the door."

"Have you been advised to retain legal counsel yet?"

"Get out of my face, Sue," Ellery warned.

She must have seen he meant it. Sue drew back, her expression wary.

"Are you sure you want to take that attitude? With or without your interview, I'm running the story—" She jumped nimbly out of the way as he slammed shut the door. From the other side of the wooden planks he heard her muffled, "Are you sure you want to do this? This is your one chance to have your side of the story heard!"

Ellery ignored her, mentally replaying his conversation with Police Chief Carson the night before. Had Carson specifically told him he was a suspect? Ellery didn't think so. But at no point had Carson told him he *wasn't* a suspect. What if the lies Sue was spreading got back to the police chief? What if Carson started to believe there was more to Ellery's final conversation with Trevor? Who *was* this eyewitness?

Ellery stepped back from the door, listening for the hoped-for sounds of Sue's retreat. He couldn't hear anything, so hopefully she had given up and was not circling the house, peering through windows.

This was unbelievable. All of it. The fact that Trevor would be murdered. The fact that Ellery would be suspected of that murder. It was like a book. Like a book *he* sold in a shop he had inherited from an eccentric aunt he'd never even known existed until she died and left him this crazy house in a crazy town where people dressed up like pirates and got themselves murdered in other people's bookshops.

Was he *dreaming*?

Ellery considered this possibility but was forced to concede he was not dreaming. So, then, what did people do in this kind of situation?

Okay, silly question.

But what should *he* do? What *could* he do?

He could call a lawyer, but that was bound to look guilty.

He could pretend this wasn't happening and carry on as normal. But normal seemed like a long time ago. He wasn't sure he still knew how normal worked.

He could do as Chief Carson asked and get him that inventory, and then he could ask Chief Carson man-to-man whether he was the only suspect in Trevor's death. Given how obnoxious Trevor had been, that seemed hard to believe. But maybe.

He would talk to the chief and figure out where things really stood. Maybe the situation wasn't as grim as Sue made it sound. Maybe it was. Either way, when he finished talking to Chief Carson—assuming he wasn't under arrest—he would call some kind of biohazard service to clean up the bloodstains in the store—Ellery paused to give his stomach a moment—and then he would call a security company to install an alarm system in the Crow's Nest, and then...

And then...

Well, he'd burn that bridge when he came to it.

CHAPTER SIX

The first stumbling block was the unwelcome news that Chief Carson was not in.

"Not in to me, or not in at all?" Ellery asked.

The baby-faced officer, whom Ellery vaguely remembered from the night before, looked puzzled. "Chief's attending the autopsy of Mr. Maples. We don't expect him back until after lunch."

Lunch and autopsy. Two words that *really* didn't go together. Ellery shuddered inwardly. "Right. Of course." He considered, said awkwardly, "I don't mean to be crass, but do you know when I'll be able to open the bookstore for business again?"

Officer Martin shook his head. "No idea. That will be the chief's call."

"Right. I just wondered what's usual in these cases."

"We don't *have* cases like this," Martin said tersely. "There is no usual."

"Sure, sure," Ellery said quickly, and then probably made it worse by adding, "Could you tell him I stopped by?" As though this had been a social call.

But after all, none of this was usual for him either.

Officer Martin gave him a look that communicated serious doubts about Ellery's solid citizen status, and Ellery headed off to put together a list of what, if anything, had been disturbed at the Crow's Nest.

He had already verified the night before that the cash register was untouched. Trevor's murder had not been part of a robbery gone wrong. But there was a slight possibility that the killer had entered the shop searching for something. The ending to a half-read mystery novel, perhaps? Yeah, no. But it didn't hurt to try and come up with a reason for someone to enter the shop after-hours. Otherwise, Ellery was liable to remain Police Chief Carson's one and only suspect.

It was probably Ellery's imagination, but the tinkle of the bell on the front door sounded almost subdued as he let himself into the building. His nose twitched at the unpleasant and unfamiliar scents of a crime scene. He glanced automatically at the red-stained floorboards where Trevor's body had lain, and then quickly away.

He dreaded the idea of being alone in the shop. Not that he imagined he was in any danger, certainly not in broad daylight, but there was no question the atmosphere felt different now, strange and unsettling.

Maybe that would change with time, but he didn't have time. The Crow's Nest hadn't exactly been bustling with business *before* it had been the scene of a homicide. Trevor's death was bound to be the death knell for the shop.

Maybe that was a selfish way of looking at things, but he had invested a lot in this little dream. And now his dream was turning into a nightmare.

"I thought it was you," someone said loudly from behind him.

Ellery jumped and whirled around. Dylan Carter, the owner of the neighboring Toy Chest, stood in the doorway. Dylan was about sixty. He was small, slim, and always impeccably dressed—today in breeches and one of those white, blousy sometimes-I-feel-like-a-pirate-sometimes-I-feel-like-a-poet shirts. His eyes were blue; his silver hair was buzzed short on the sides, and the top—when not tied back in a bandanna—fell in a stylishly long swoop.

"What does *that* mean?" Ellery protested. Dylan was the closest thing Ellery had to a friend in Pirate's Cove, so this accusation cut deeply. "I had nothing to do with it!"

Dylan looked taken aback. "Of course not. No one thinks *that*. I meant I recognized you going past the window of my store."

"*Oh.*" Ellery flushed. Nothing like a guilty conscience—especially when you weren't guilty. "I just… The editor of the local paper practically accused me to my face of murdering Trevor. I'm a little touchy."

"Sue? Sue did that? That's terrible." Dylan seemed genuinely shocked. "That doesn't sound like Sue." His gaze moved past Ellery to the stained floor. His tanned face seemed to lose color. "Is that where it happened?"

"I don't know where it happened, but that's where I found him," Ellery said.

They stared in silence at the gruesome brown-red patch in the center of the floor.

Dylan shook his head. "It's unbelievable."

"I know."

"Do the police have any theories?"

"I'm just a suspect. Chief Carson didn't share his theories with me."

Dylan's eyes widened. "But you can't *really* be a suspect."

"I kind of think I am," Ellery admitted.

"But that's ridiculous. You barely knew the man. There are plenty of better suspects than you in this town."

"Like who?"

Dylan hesitated just long enough for Ellery to wonder what his relationship with Trevor had been like. Dylan said, "Tommy Rider for one."

Ellery was taken aback. "The real-estate agent?"

"The same. And Janet Maples. Trevor's ex-wife. That was a very ugly divorce. *Oh*, and let's not forget Cyrus. He and Trevor fought about everything from zoning permits to signage—and that was *before* Trevor decided to run for mayor." Dylan's smile was wide and without guile. "For that matter, I won't be shedding any tears over Trevor."

If Dylan was trying to cheer Ellery up with this list of people who might have wanted Trevor out of the way, he was succeeding. "Why's that?"

"The theater where the Scallywags perform goes up for sale next month, and Trevor had already told me he intended to bid against me."

In addition to owning next door's Toy Chest, a tiny but charming toys and games shop, Dylan ran the local amateur theater guild known as the Scallywags. He kept trying to get Ellery to join, but Ellery was only too aware of his limitations as an actor. He had the reviews to prove it.

"That's a relief. I was starting to get the feeling everyone believed I was—I had—"

"Of course not," Dylan said staunchly. "Anyone who knew Trevor knows perfectly well there's a mile-long list of suspects." His gaze returned to the stained floor as though he couldn't help himself. "Are you open today? Because you'll probably want to do something about...that..."

"Ugh. No. I'm supposed to make a list of anything that's missing or damaged for Chief Carson."

Dylan looked thoughtful. "The chief thinks someone broke in here and Trevor spotted them and came to investigate? That does sound like Trevor."

No, it didn't. Not to Ellery. Granted, he hadn't known Trevor that well. And the opposite scenario was equally unlikely. If Trevor or someone else had wanted something out of the Crow's Nest, they would surely have taken it after Great-great-great-aunt Eudora died and before Ellery had taken possession. There would have been ample opportunity.

Speaking of opportunity.

"You didn't happen to see anything out of the ordinary yesterday evening?" Ellery asked. "The police think Trevor was killed between five and seven, so..."

Dylan winced. "No. The police already questioned me about that. The thing is, with it being the start of Buccaneer Days, I decided to close early and get over to the theater." He looked apologetic. "From what I understand, Sandy closed early too."

Sandy ran the small art gallery on the other side the Crow's Nest.

Ellery said, "I thought Buccaneer Days was supposed to boost business for all of us?"

"Maybe eventually. Right now, it's mostly for the village's own amusement."

That was certainly how it had looked in the Salty Dog last evening. And it was probably one reason Chief Carson hadn't even seemed to consider the possibility Trevor had been killed by a non-resident.

Ellery said, "Speaking of village amusements, do you have any idea who I could call to get these bloodstains out?"

"Out Damn Spot," Dylan replied promptly. "Their motto is: *Your secrets are our secret.* Tell them I referred you."

At first glance, nothing appeared to be missing from the Crow's Nest.

Ellery checked the locked case with first editions by Elizabeth Peters and Ian Fleming. Undoubtedly the most valuable items in the shop. The books sat undisturbed and already slightly dusty again, behind glass.

He checked the small collection of vintage bookends—great little ready-made murder weapons sitting all in a row—but every single bookend was unbloodied and accounted for.

He checked the erotic mystery section because, hey, you never know.

After that, he got distracted by phoning the cleaning company and then phoning the alarm company.

The cleaning service turned out to be co-owned by Dylan and run by his niece, which, in Ellery's opinion, explained the whimsical company name. Pandora promised to be at the Crow's Nest first thing Monday morning, mop in hand. The folks at the alarm company were equally helpful—news of murder in Pirate's Cove had already reached them—and they answered all Ellery's questions and then set up an appointment for Monday to quote new security systems for both the Crow's Nest and Captain's Seat.

By then it was after one, and Ellery felt a little more on top of things than he had that morning. He had spoken to Sandy next door, and she had reaffirmed Dylan's assurances that no one seriously believed Ellery was a suspect in Trevor's murder.

He wanted to believe her. Maybe he had misread Chief Carson's tone the night before? Maybe Chief Carson treated everyone to that brusque, skeptical manner.

Anyway, the good news was his neighbors did not believe him capable of homicide. The bad news was that for all he knew, the bookshop might have to remain closed for the duration of the investigation. With the Crow's Nest closed, Ellery had no income to keep the store afloat or himself from going broke. He needed the case to come to a quick resolution—one that did not end with his arrest—so that he could make the most of whatever business Buccaneer Days brought in.

Since sitting around worrying never solved anything, he decided to head back to Captain's Seat and take his frustrations out on the kitchen's remaining linoleum. He was on the wooden walk outside the shop, trying to get the door to lock, when Chief Carson pulled up in a white SUV with blue and gold insignia.

Ellery waited, trying to quash his unease as the chief unfolded from the vehicle and crossed the pavement. With an expression that unrevealing, Carson was probably a wiz at poker. Heck, he was probably a wiz at Russian roulette.

"Hi," Ellery called.

"I understand you stopped by the station earlier," Carson said. Not one for idle chitchat, clearly.

"Yes. I did." He still wanted to ask Carson if he was the main suspect in Trevor's murder, but even a few months in Pirate's Cove had taught Ellery the walls had ears. Possibly also the doors, windows, and flower boxes.

Speaking of doors, he was still having trouble getting this one to lock. He pulled his key out, turned the knob, and the wretched thing swung open again. He felt vaguely flustered—and irritated by his reaction—as Carson reached him.

Carson looked just as grim up close as he did from a distance. Or maybe grim wasn't the correct word. Stern? Stoic? Severe? He did not look like someone who smiled much, put it that way. Of course, being a cop was bound to be serious work, especially a cop with a murder to solve, but the pre-homicide Carson hadn't been noticeably cheerier.

"Were you able to determine if anything's missing from the store?" Carson asked.

The wind off the ocean ruffled his sun-streaked hair. Ellery caught a hint of manly scents: soap, shampoo, and single-mindedness. Also possibly a splash of Jack Black Post Shave Cooling Gel and Aftershave. Todd had worn it too, and the familiarity of the fragrance triggered an unsettling Pavlovian response in him.

What was the term for that? Psychic secretion? Yikes. And why was he thinking about secretions, psychic or otherwise, at a time like this?

Ellery said quickly, talking himself away from his wayward imagination, "I didn't notice anything missing. I mean, I didn't conduct a full inventory, but I checked all the obvious things."

He jammed the key back in the lock, twisted it impatiently, tried the knob…and the door opened. He exhaled sharply.

Carson watched him without comment. Or rather, his only comment was, "What are all the obvious things?"

"No money was missing, no first editions…" Ellery shoved the door shut, jammed the key in, twisted left, twisted right—

"Is there a problem with the door?" Carson asked, which was a rhetorical question if there ever was one.

Ellery huffed his exasperation, straightened, and glared at the chief. "Why no. Why do you ask?"

Sarcasm bounced off Carson like bullets off Superman. "Let's step inside," he said.

Ellery opened the door, pushed it wide for the chief, who stepped past him. He got another whiff of aftershave. The old floorboards creaked beneath the chief's boots. Once again Ellery felt obliged to fill his uncomfortable awareness of the other man—the other *married* man—with chatter.

"I called a local company this afternoon, and tomorrow they're going to rekey and give me a quote for installing a security system. Hopefully, they'll fix the door while they're here."

Carson turned to face him. "I hope you're joking."

"About what?" Ellery asked warily.

"This is still technically a crime scene."

"I know that."

"You know that..."

"It's not like I'm opening for business. But I can't leave the building unprotected. Look what happened yesterday. I have to be able to secure the building."

"The building *was* secured," Carson said. "I locked this door myself last night. If there's a problem now—"

"If there's a problem now *what*?" Ellery challenged him. But yeah, of course Carson would have no problem locking up. Even inanimate hardware wouldn't have the audacity to defy the chief of police.

Carson stared him down with those hard, bright eyes. All he said was, "Let's take a look at the lock."

"Be my guest." Ellery stepped out of the way.

Carson knelt to examine the lock, turning the bronze handle this way and that. "Do you have any graphite?"

"I've tried graphite a couple of times. I need a more permanent solution." He added bitterly, "Maybe an ax."

"For now, let's use graphite."

Ellery went to fetch the graphite. When he returned, Carson had the entire handle dismantled, pieces neatly laid out on the floor.

It was kind of disconcerting seeing someone as dignified and authoritative as Carson was in his navy-blue uniform, crawling around the floor. Well, not crawling. More of a tidy scoot from position to position.

"Okay, I see the problem here." He pointed a small Phillips head screwdriver because OF COURSE HE WOULD HAVE ONE. He probably had a utility belt like Batman, hidden somewhere on his person. "You've got about a decade's worth of sea salt and grime gumming up the works." He held his hand out for the tube of graphite, which Ellery handed over.

"So I guess having the bloodstains on the floor cleaned up is also a no-no," Ellery said, watching Carson's long, nimble fingers lubricate the lock pieces and then quickly reassemble the handle.

Carson's lashes flicked up, and he gave Ellery a thoughtful look before directing his attention back to the door handle. "You can have the floor cleaned as soon as we release the crime scene."

"Which is going to be when?"

"When I say so." Carson finished turning the last of the screws, fastening the faceplate securely. He closed the door, turned the knob, turned the button, nodded in satisfaction. "That'll work for now." He rose, dusted off his knees. "I did tell you to get that lock replaced."

"I know. You did." Ellery dreaded asking, but he had to know. "Look, I can't— I have to— Am I *really* a suspect in Trevor Maples's death?"

Carson made a sound that fell somewhere between laugh and snort. "Of course you're a suspect. You're my *main* suspect."

CHAPTER SEVEN

"**B**ut I *can't* be."

Carson looked interested. "Why can't you be?"

"Because… Well, first of all, because I barely knew Trevor. Which means, how could I have a motive?"

"We've yet to determine how well you and Maples knew each other. That's what background checks are for. Which means, we don't yet know whether you have motive or not."

"But—"

Carson kept talking. "What we do know is that Maples's body was found in *your* bookstore by *you*, following an argument earlier in the day with *you*."

"I can't be the only person with a motive."

"True."

"Or the only person Trevor argued with."

"As far as we can determine, you're the only person Maples argued with on the day of his death. And yes, while there are others with grudges against our victim, those were long-standing grievances. I can't ignore the fact that you showed up in Pirate's Cove and shortly after, Maples ended up dead."

"I don't believe this." Ellery closed his eyes, took a couple of deep breaths, opened his eyes and glared. "Are you even *looking* at anyone else?"

"I just told you we were."

"Because according to Sue Lewis, I'm the only suspect."

"Sue Lewis? What does Sue have to do with anything?"

"She came to my house today, wanting an interview with the prime suspect."

Carson shrugged. "She didn't get that from my department. But it's a logical deduction."

"Great."

Carson studied him. "You're not going to be railroaded. We're going to conduct a fair and thorough investigation. A man has been murdered. We owe him and every other citizen of Pirate's Cove no less."

Ellery nodded. His throat was too tight for words. He understood what the chief was saying, and if his own situation wasn't so precarious, maybe he could have accepted things more stoically. But as it was…

"I'm barely hanging on now." He tried to keep his voice steady, but his words were embarrassingly husky. "The shop, I mean. If I'm forced to stay closed, I'm finished. I'm probably finished anyway. No one is going to want to come into a place where a murder happened." He had to stop. He could feel Carson's gaze, though he avoided meeting it. Finally, he shrugged, got out, "Okay, well, is that it? Can we go?"

"The list," Carson reminded him.

Ellery's temper came to his rescue. "There is no list! I told you that. Nothing was taken. Everything is exactly as I left it."

"You still can't think of any reason for Maples to come back in here last night?"

"No!"

"Because that's the key piece of evidence against you." Carson sounded impatient again. "The body was found in *your* place of business by *you*. That's two strikes."

"I don't care if it's a hundred strikes. I didn't have anything to do with this!"

"Why *did* you come back last night?"

Ellery looked ceilingward. "We've covered this how many times? I had to get my car. I was parked in the back."

"But why did you come into the shop?"

Ellery was still gazing upward, past Chief Carson's head, past the top of the doorframe. He answered mechanically, "The lights were on. I could see them from the sidewalk."

Carson glanced behind himself, glanced at Ellery, followed Ellery's fixed gaze to the two empty hooks in the wall above the door.

"Something wrong?"

Ellery swallowed. "I-I just noticed. Something *is* missing."

"What?"

He pointed. "The pirate sword above the door."

Carson repeated without inflection, "The pirate sword."

Ellery said quickly, "It wasn't real. I mean, it was real, but not an antique. It was a replica. I don't think it was valuable or anything."

Carson said nothing, continuing to eye him with that unrevealing gaze.

One reason Ellery had not been a very good actor was because he was not a very good liar. He was by nature a little too forthcoming, a little too free-spoken. But only an idiot could fail to see that his already delicate position as most-likely-to-wind-up-with-an-inmate-number was about to get even dicier.

"It was just a typical pirate sword. A short, wide, double-edged blade, basket-shaped hilt—"

"A cutlass." Carson spoke with bleak certainty. "That makes sense."

It did? But why? Why did Carson sound like that? Why was he giving him that look? Why did it make Ellery's position so much worse if someone had broken in to steal the sword? It wasn't like—

Realization swept over him. Ellery sucked in a breath, said faintly, "But I thought he was shot…"

"Did you?" Carson said grimly.

"Yes! Of course. You mean you knew last night he wasn't shot?"

"I've seen enough gunshot wounds to know one when I see it."

"I haven't."

Carson said nothing.

"I didn't know," Ellery insisted.

"You didn't know Maples was stabbed to death, and you didn't notice the sword was gone, even though it hangs right over the front door and even though you said you searched for anything missing or out of place."

When he put it like that…

"I don't know what to tell you. It was there yesterday afternoon. I'm positive about that. It fell down when Trevor slammed the door—"

"Slammed the door," repeated Carson. "So it *was* a heated argument."

"I already told you he was annoyed because I didn't want to sell him the bookshop. He was a door-slamming kind of person. That doesn't prove anything."

Oh no. Wherever that sword was, Ellery's fingerprints were going to be all over it. He thought quickly, said, "For God's sake, Chief. If I was going to kill Trevor, wouldn't I need a better reason than he was starting to annoy me? And would I do it in my own shop? With my own sword? And then calmly go to dinner? I'd have to be crazy."

"Maybe you *are* crazy. Who knows? You're an outsider here."

It shouldn't have hurt because it was perfectly true. Somehow it did.

Ellery shook his head. He had no idea what to say. The missing sword. The dead body. All of this happening in his little bookshop. It was like a movie. The kind of movie he hated—along with war movies, prison movies, and animals-with-a-quest movies. How was this his life now?

"Where's the sword?" Carson demanded harshly. "Don't lie to me. *Where is it?*"

Ellery stared at him stupidly.

"Where did you hide it?"

"I-I didn't."

"Page, I can't help you if you don't help me. Where. Is. The. Sword?"

"How. Should. I. Know?" Ellery rapped back.

Carson continued to glower. Ellery scowled right back.

Was he supposed to melt into a guilty puddle beneath Carson's steely gaze? Because that wasn't going to happen. Yes, he was scared and worried, but he was also indignant at being judged so unfairly.

Maybe Carson saw that, saw Ellery's mounting defiance, because some of the ferocity in his posture eased. When he spoke again, his tone was less abrasive. "Okay, let's say you didn't kill Maples. Let's say, for the sake of argument, you came back from dinner last night, found him on the floor with the sword beside him, realized how it would look, and hid it."

Did anybody really fall for that pseudo-sincere help-me-help-you schtick?

"Your officers searched the store last night," Ellery said. "Was the sword here?"

"Last night we thought we were looking for a knife, maybe a machete. We didn't conduct the kind of search we're going to conduct if you don't produce that weapon in the next five seconds."

The threat was not implied; it was thrown down right there in the open like a gauntlet.

"Go ahead and search. I don't know what else to tell you. Maybe the killer, who is not and has never been me, took it away with them."

He knew Carson didn't believe him. Maybe in Carson's position he wouldn't believe him either. But if the chief wasn't even going to try to find another suspect, Ellery would have to do it for him. Carson was right. Ellery was a stranger in Pirate's Cove. He had no history, good or bad, no one could vouch for him, probably no one would even care if he ended up being arrested and convicted. That was the way the world worked. Everybody was busy with their own thing. Even people in small towns, where he had imagined it might be different.

It wasn't different.

Worst of all, if he was arrested for this crime, the real murderer would likely rejoice. And that was the most galling part of all, because he couldn't help feeling this was personal. Someone had deliberately dragged him into this murder. Used his shop, used his sword, used his difficulties with Trevor to, well, frame him.

He waited for Chief Carson to say the magic words: *you're under arrest.*

It was so quiet in the Crow's Nest, he could hear the clock in the Romantic Suspense section tick-tock-tick-tock-ing each second.

Carson continued to eye him, somber and silent.

What was he waiting for?

Just as Ellery was thinking he understood why, under the strain of interrogation, innocent people made false confessions, Carson said suddenly, crisply, "Very well. If that's the way you want to play it."

"That's the way it is."

Unimpressed, Carson handed over a business card. "If you remember something you believe would be useful in your defense, you can reach me at any of these numbers."

Ellery stared down at the rows of tiny numbers. He nodded.

Carson turned, opened the door, and left.

The shop felt very large and weirdly empty after his departure.

CHAPTER EIGHT

Ellery stared down at the card he held.

It was kind of shattering to have someone gaze deep into your eyes and decide you were one of the bad guys.

Especially when you were one of the good guys. Or at least one of the normal, average, decent guys. One of the guys who wouldn't resort to murder as a means of solving his problems.

And here he'd been thinking Todd cheating on him with Jerry was the worst thing he could go through. Man, had he got it wrong.

Great-great-great-aunt Eudora's gift was coming with some unexpected strings attached. Strings that were starting to look alarmingly like handcuffs. So okay. He would not wait docilely to be thrown in the hoosegow by Sheriff Jack. He was going to prove his innocence to this town, if it was the last thing he did. He just needed to find where that sword had gone, and he'd know who really was behind all this. How hard could that be?

If there was one thing life had taught him, it was that people talked.

Whether they were gossiping about your cheating boyfriend or speculating on who might have reason to commit murder, people could be relied on to blab. Very well. It would be Ellery's job to be a good and proactive listener.

Whoever had done this had to have a motive. *Ipso facto*, he just had to figure out who stood to gain the most by Trevor's death. It had to be something pretty major to drive someone to murder, right? Not just that, though. Who stood to benefit by pinning Trevor's murder on *him*? Because that had to be an important element in all this. The decision to frame Ellery couldn't be random or spontaneous. No one had grabbed that sword on impulse. For one thing, they couldn't have reached it without a ladder or stepstool.

Did that mean premeditation?

The only problem was, he couldn't think of anyone other than Trevor who had anything to gain by him being in trouble with the law—and if this was Trevor's plan, it was a terrible one. But it was true. No one but Trevor had ever shown any interest in buying the Crow's Nest. The bookshop was not and had never been a thriving concern even though it was situated on a prime piece of real estate.

Location helped, but it was not everything.

Well, maybe the point of framing him wasn't personal. Maybe it was because someone had to take the fall, and why not Ellery? He was an outsider, he was conveniently located, and he had a somewhat contentious relationship with the victim.

But, according to Dylan, there were others with equally—or maybe even more—contentious relationships with Trevor. Including Dylan himself. Although it was really hard to picture affable, dapper Dylan committing murder. Especially in such a violent fashion.

Still, he would have to be considered. Along with the other cast of characters. Ellery would see what he could find out about each one of these other potential suspects: the ex-wife, the rival candidates for mayor…and there had to be others. Trevor had been an obnoxious personality. He was bound to have other enemies.

He contemplated the lock on the front door. Had it really not occurred to Chief Carson how easy it would be for someone to pick that lock? Heck, never mind picking it, they probably could have just given it a hard wiggle.

Come to think of it, did anyone have a spare key to the Crow's Nest? He recalled something in one of the emails from Tommy Rider about Great-great-great-aunt Eudora giving a spare key to someone because the older woman sometimes forgot her own keys.

He would have to go through his emails and confirm that. In fact, wouldn't Tommy have a key? She was the real-estate agent handling the property. Surely, she would have to have a key.

Whoa.

Tommy had just jumped to the top of his list of suspects. Except it was as hard to picture bubbly, flirtatious Tommy committing murder as it was imagining Dylan. Especially a premeditated crime. That had to require a certain coldness, a certain calculation that not everyone was capable of.

Also, how hard was it to run someone through with a sword?

Would it take a stronger than average woman?

Something else he would need to figure out.

In the meantime, he needed a little break from murder and mayhem. He needed to focus on something he could actually control. Something that made more sense than the situation he found himself in.

With the Crow's Nest safely (fingers crossed) locked up, Ellery made his way to the hardware store. In addition to a new floor, which he could not yet afford, the kitchen at Captain's Seat desperately needed a new coat of paint, and he needed to get some other supplies to help with the remodel of the mansion.

It was almost a relief to have the distraction of the old house. At least one thing in his life could be torn apart and put back together to be much better than before.

Hardware and More was the only hardware store in town. It was also one of the longest-running businesses in Pirate's Cove. As one of the first legit enterprises to go up in the small seaside village, the proprietors showed extra enthusiasm in celebrating Buccaneer Days. Ellery felt like he was stepping back in time when he walked through the doors. Not only were the workers dressed up in their olden-days costumes, but so was the store kitted out in swashbuckling memorabilia meant to transport customers back in time.

It just went to show home improvement was not a modern development.

Ellery wandered down the paint aisle, considering shades and hues. The names of some of the colors were pretty entertaining: "Memory Lane," "Lost in the Mist," "Silverpointe"... Maybe a gray-blue accent wall in the dining room? Maybe green-blue walls in the kitchen?

He was thinking how closely "Clear Vista" matched Chief Carson's eyes when a middle-aged man dressed in a greatcoat and tricorn hat bumped into him. The man dropped his blunderbuss on Ellery's foot.

"Ouch," said Ellery, steadying himself against the paint shelves.

"Good heavens! I'm so sorry. I'm afraid I was daydreaming." The man stooped, snatched up his short-barreled shotgun, and offered an apologetic smile. His cocoa-colored eyes widened as they met Ellery's. "Mayor Cyrus Jones, at your service. And you, if I'm not mistaken, are Ellery Page, our newest resident." The mayor stuck out a beringed hand for Ellery to shake.

Ellery, grateful for a little friendliness, smiled back as he shook hands. "Nice to meet you."

Jones had a firm but surprisingly gentle handshake. Beneath the blue tricorn hat, his face was chubby and clean-shaven; the wrinkles around his eyes gave away his age, but also indicated someone who laughed often and deeply. He had that elusively contemporary look some people have, but his costume fit like it was tailor-made for him.

A can of bright purple paint sat in his basket—"Unimaginable" according to the color chart—and the mayor beamed, catching Ellery's gaze.

"My tweenaged granddaughter Elsie is visiting us this summer, and she wants her room to be purple."

"She ought to love that shade."

"I'm sure she will." His expression grew kind and concerned. "And how are you holding up?"

"Well," Ellery said. That was actually a start and not a statement, but he couldn't think of anything to add. *Prime suspect* was such a weird and unbelievable situation to find himself in.

"Under the circumstances, eh?" Jones's smile was sympathetic.

"Under the circumstances, yes." They were getting a few curious glances from other costume-clad customers, and Ellery's face warmed.

"Don't you worry, my boy, Chief Carson will have this mess cleaned up in no time."

"Sure," Ellery said without conviction.

If the mayor heard his doubt, he gave no sign. "I don't believe any nephew of Eudora Page is capable of such a heinous act. The Pages were always good people. Solid citizens."

"Great." How much was that worth? He really knew nothing about his father's side of the family. His father had died when Ellery was a baby, and his mother had remarried when Ellery turned eight. He had always thought of George, his stepfather, as Dad.

"And in any case, between you and me, you're not the only suspect." Jones winked. "Do you have a sense of humor?"

"I hope so."

"People all over the village are making bets on who the most likely suspect is. You're not the only person Trevor rubbed the wrong way."

Yeah, that wasn't all that humorous really, but Ellery tried not to let his dismay show.

"Who's the current odds-on favorite?" He couldn't help recalling that Dylan had considered Jones a potential suspect, given that Trevor had been beating him in the mayoral race. Yesterday Trevor had been beating Jones and Tommy Rider both.

"It's a four-way tie." The mayor laughed cheerfully and dropped his blunderbuss again.

This time Ellery moved his foot in time.

The mayor muttered something that sounded like, "Boil it in oil." He once more picked up his gun, shoved it in his overly tight bandolier—where it nearly popped out again.

"Uh, that's not loaded, is it?" Ellery asked. The stares other shoppers were throwing them indicated a shared concern.

"No, no," the mayor said breezily. "It hasn't been fired in years."

Ellery swallowed.

"Anyway, what was I saying? Oh, a four-way tie. That's right. True, yours is the most practical motive."

"Is it? It is?"

"Of course. Scuttlebutt has it that Trevor wanted to buy your store, and so you took out the competition before he could take *you* out."

"What about the other suspects' motives?"

The mayor looked thoughtful. "As ambitious as Thomasina is, she's smart enough to know that in the end, I'm going to be reelected. And though Janet is still bitter about the divorce settlement, it's hard to imagine her waiting five years to exact her revenge. Besides, they say poison is a woman's weapon, and that seems right to me. If Janet had been going to murder Trevor, she'd have told him she was ready to sell her share in the bookstore, invite him over to discuss terms, and make him a nice cup of poisoned tea." Jones's warm eyes twinkled with amusement.

Ellery? Not so much.

"I didn't realize Trevor shared ownership of Gimcrack Antiques."

"They don't share ownership. Didn't." Jones seemed puzzled. "Oh, you mean the bookstore? Entirely different enterprise. It's one reason Trevor wanted your shop so badly. He couldn't get Janet to hand over Old Salt Stationery. She owned the store before they married, you see."

"You mean, the woman who owns the place on Mizzen Street is Trevor's ex-wife? I never made the connection." He also hadn't considered that shop to be anything but a stationery store, though now that he thought about it, they did sell magazines and current paperback bestsellers. His eyes widened at the idea of that tall, very thin, very severe-looking woman ever being married to someone as loud and vulgar as Trevor.

"That's right," Jones said. "But my money is on your neighbor, Dylan Carter. Carter is dead set on buying the old theater on Wallace Street and so was Trevor. And neither of those two were ever good losers."

"That's… Well, at least I'm not the only person of interest." Ellery didn't know if this wealth of gossipy information made him feel better or worse, but at least he had a more solid starting point for his own inquiry.

Jones said, "Not by a long shot, my boy. Don't let the gossips and naysayers get you down. The truth will come out. The truth always comes out." He smiled and patted Ellery on the shoulder as he moved past with his basket of purple paint.

Ellery returned a weak smile and went back to perusing color samples.

After picking out an elegant ivory he thought would work for the dining room, he left the hardware store.

He was loading cans of paint and other supplies into his VW when a deep and vaguely familiar voice called out, "Avast there, me bucko!"

A throbbing pain sliced through his head, but he fastened a smile to his face, turned and saw Tommy Rider coming his way.

"Hey there. Long time, no see!"

Tommy grinned. Today's ensemble was full-on pirate drag: a pink brocade coat, tightly fitted black breeches, lacy white shirt, and tall black boots. Her hair was a mass of wild curls. She held a box of chandelier light bulbs, though he hadn't noticed her in the hardware store.

"Are you out on bail or on the lam?"

"Ha," Ellery said. "Neither." If people could joke about your guilt, did that mean they didn't *really* suspect you? Maybe? Hopefully?

Tommy reached him. "Why aren't you in costume?"

Ellery glanced down at his jeans and T-shirt. "I just came into town to pick up a few things."

Tommy wiggled her eyebrows. "Tight breeches. Bare chest. Pirate hat. You'd have more business than you'd know what to do with."

"Yeah, I really don't—"

"I'm just teasing you. Seriously, how are you holding up, kiddo?"

Kiddo? She was at most ten years older than him. But the concern in her eyes seemed genuine, and Ellery felt some of his tension ease. It was not a lot of fun feeling like Public Enemy Number One. Though no one in the hardware store other than Mayor Jones had accosted him, he had been uncomfortably aware of the stares and whispers that followed him down every aisle.

"I'm okay. A little shell-shocked," he admitted.

"You and everyone else. Though if anyone in this town had to be eliminated, I guess Trevor was a good first draft pick." She shrugged at Ellery's expression. "One thing I'm not is a hypocrite."

"I can see that."

"I think the police department is really dragging their butts on this one," Tommy said. "There should have been an arrest by now."

"I can't say I mind, since I'm probably the person most likely to be arrested."

Tommy laughed. "You? Why would you think that? Janet Maples is who Chief Carson ought to throw behind bars. But she used to work for the police department, so of course they want to look the other way."

"Janet Maples? The ex-wife? Why do you think she would kill Trevor? Didn't they divorce a long time ago?"

"It's always the wife. Don't you watch *Law and Order*?"

"I'm not a fan of mysteries."

Tommy looked taken aback at this admission, and then burst out laughing. "Then why the h-e-double-toothpick are you running a mystery bookstore?"

"Because I inherited it."

"You mean if you'd inherited a bakery, you'd be making cupcakes right now?"

"I love cupcakes," Ellery admitted.

Tommy laughed. "Oh my God, that's so funny. Well, here's the scoop, matey. Janet and Trevor had a *tumultuous* relationship, and things have remained tense ever since their split. In fact, I've never known a nastier divorce, and I work in real estate!"

"But why would Janet wait years to get even?"

"*That's* what the police need to find out. Janet should be brought in for questioning and arrested. It's an open-and-shut case, if you ask me. As potential future mayor, I plan on lighting a fire under the police department when it comes to investigations like this." Tommy offered a charming smile with her impromptu campaign pitch.

"Do you think there'll be a lot of future cases like this?"

Tommy shrugged. "Er, no. But that's not the point."

Ellery gave an unwilling laugh. "Good. I'd hate to think I'd moved to Cabot Cove by mistake."

"See, you do like mysteries!"

"Nope. But my mother loves Angela Lansbury. Anyway, I appreciate the kind words. I just hope the killer is brought to justice soon. I think everyone forgets that while their attention is focused on me, a murderer is walking around Pirate's Cove." Ellery slammed shut the trunk and moved toward the driver's door.

Tommy looked thoughtful. "Good point. Leave it to an innocent person to think of that."

Ellery tried to look appropriately innocent.

Tommy said, "I think I'm going to go have a chat with Chief Carson. This situation really needs to be taken seriously."

He could have told her Carson took it plenty seriously, but he was tired and ready to head home—while he was still free to do so.

He unlocked the door, opened it, and a thought occurred. "Tommy?"

She was already halfway down the sidewalk, but she glanced back. "Yes?"

"You emailed me a while back that Great-great-great-aunt Eudora had given a spare key to the Crow's Nest to someone. Do you remember who?"

Tommy's light eyes widened. He saw her processing his question, saw a flicker of wariness cross her face, but then she smiled. "Sure. Dylan Carter had a spare key. I don't know if he still does. Probably." She winked. "Enjoy your day, Ellery." She sauntered off, hips swaying, dark curls bouncing in the sea breeze.

CHAPTER NINE

"**Y**ou still here? I thought you were closed on Sundays," Dylan greeted as Ellery walked into the Toy Chest.

"I'm just about to head home." Ellery had been trying to think of a tactful way to ask about the spare key, but since nothing had come to him, he just went for it. "Hey, I wanted to ask if you still have a key to the Crow's Nest?"

Dylan had been tying price tags to the masts of a small fleet of fiberglass sailboats. He froze for an instant and his expression went blank. "A key?"

"Right."

Dylan hesitated. "I don't think…" he began.

Ellery cut in, "When Tommy and I were first communicating about the property, she mentioned Great-great-great-aunt Eudora had given you a spare key."

"Oh, *right*!" Dylan said with false heartiness. The alarm in his eyes was plain even across the room. "I'd forgotten all about that key. Yes. Eudora did give me a key ages ago. I don't think I've seen it in years." As if in afterthought, he asked, "Why? Did you want it back?"

Ellery understood Dylan's dilemma. Even if he was perfectly innocent—and Ellery wanted to believe he was—Dylan knew having that key in his possession upped his standing as a suspect in Trevor's murder. Of course it did! Because one of the things that made Ellery's own position so perilous was the location of the crime scene. The fact that Trevor had been found in Ellery's closed store was one of the biggest counts against him.

But with a flimsy front-door lock and spare keys floating around, that particular indicator of guilt carried a lot less weight. Reasonable doubt. That was the name of the game, and the fact that the Crow's Nest was more easily accessible than it might appear at first glance, certainly created reasonable doubt. At least on that score.

"It doesn't matter. I'm having the place rekeyed tomorrow."

"Ah," Dylan said. "Of course."

Ellery wasn't enjoying this. He liked Dylan. He'd liked Dylan from the moment Dylan had first strolled into the bookstore to tell him that the local theater was doing an adaptation of *Peter Pan* and would he like complimentary tickets.

Through the cold and wet spring they had bonded over a mutual love of theater, the *New Yorker*, cocktails, and kitsch. Dylan had made Ellery feel welcome. He had made him feel he could add value to the community. While most of the village might whisper behind Ellery's back, he had known Dylan would never join in. It was painful to realize Dylan was lying to him.

And it wasn't like he could challenge him on it.

Awkwardly, Ellery said, "Okay. I just wondered."

Dylan was equally uncomfortable. "No need to worry. That key's safe in the back of a drawer somewhere." He was still smiling that stiff, strained smile.

"See you tomorrow," Ellery said, and practically backed out of the store.

* * * * *

MURDER HE WROUGHT!

Ellery spat his morning coffee all over the front page of the *Scuttlebutt Weekly* as he read the Monday morning headline.

Failed actor, failed screenwriter, and now failed bookseller Ellery Page may have finally succeeded at one thing. The New York transplant is the prime suspect in the murder of one of Pirate's Cove leading citizens, according to a source at PCPD.

What had he ever done to Sue Lewis—to anyone, for that matter—to deserve this treatment?

His disbelieving gaze raked over each malicious sentence, pausing only to goggle in outrage at the very unflattering photo of himself looking half-crazed—with bits of linoleum in his hair, no less—taken yesterday morning when he'd snarled at Sue Lewis to get out of his face—and doorway.

What a-a...piece of work! Lewis *and* her paper. This wasn't journalism, it was a hatchet job. It was a hit piece. It was character assassination. And, by the way, wasn't it illegal to publish a photo of someone without their consent? He would have to ask his lawyer. Did he have a lawyer? Did Mr. Landry count as his lawyer, or had his responsibilities ended with Great-great-great-aunt Eudora? Anyway, he would have to ask a lawyer about this and about other things, because the article made it sound like he was about to be arrested any second.

Was he?

Ellery's heart sank. He had actually been feeling almost cheerful when he arrived at work that morning. When Chief Carson had phoned late last night to tell him he could reopen the shop, Ellery had assumed that was a good sign. Not that Carson had put it that way, but he had said the final survey of the bookshop had been conducted and the Crow's Nest was being released as a crime scene.

"What does that mean?" Ellery had asked.

"It means we've got everything we need from the crime scene," Carson had replied.

Maybe he'd meant they now had enough to charge Ellery?

It sure sounded that way from Sue's article.

He sucked in a sharp breath. Was it possible they had searched the shop again and discovered the sword hidden somewhere?

According to eyewitness accounts, Page repeatedly threatened Maples, the leading candidate in the closely contested race for mayor of Pirate's Cove.

That wasn't even true. He hadn't repeatedly threatened Trevor. He hadn't threatened him at all. And what eyewitness accounts? There had been no eyewitnesses.

Wait.

Ellery stopped, thinking back. Come to think of it, there *had* been someone in the store during at least part of his argument with Trevor. That person had departed by the time Ellery rehung the cutlass over the door, because Ellery vaguely remembered glancing down the aisles of shelves for him. Or her.

His heart began to pound with a mix of alarm and excitement. He needed to know who this "eyewitness" was because it seemed very possible to him that here was another suspect in Trevor's murder.

Or was he jumping to conclusions?

He wasn't sure. Just because you jumped to a conclusion didn't mean your conclusion was wrong.

Anyway, he needed to know who that unseen listener was. And he also wanted to know who the unnamed source was at Pirate's Cove Police Department—and whether it was true he was about to be arrested.

According to persons familiar with the case, Maples had offered to purchase the failing business on two separate occasions. Page, who inherited the store from lifelong PICO resident and local eccentric Eudora Page, became enraged and accused Maples of trying to drive him out of business.

How could someone get away with printing such a pack of lies? And also—off-topic but true—man, he hated that kind of cutesy acronym. Just spell out the name of the village for heaven's sake! Jeez.

He finished the article and rested his face in his hands. Every time he thought things were getting better, they got worse. Every time he thought things were as bad as they could get, they got worse. Was he never going to catch a break? The hit piece in the *Scuttlebutt Weekly* felt like the last straw. According to Lewis's reporting, Ellery was the only real suspect in Trevor's murder—and that might even be true—but what was worse, much worse, was the unsubtle suggestion that Ellery was indeed guilty of the crime. Lewis wasn't just accusing him, she pretty much had him already tried and convicted.

The awful part was people would believe it. *He'd* believe it, if he were reading about someone else. He'd take it for granted the paper was unbiased. He was shocked that it wasn't. Was this just a small-town thing? Someone had to be guilty and he was the outsider? Or was Lewis so desperate to boost circulation that she was willing to exaggerate the facts and slant the news? Or was it something else? Something personal.

It felt personal, but that was likely because he was the target.

Ellery lowered his hands. He couldn't know Sue Lewis's motivation, but one thing he could find out was how much truth there was to her story. If there was one person in PICO—

er, Pirate's Cove—who didn't mind sharing unvarnished and painful truths, it was Jack Carson.

Ellery rose from his desk, grabbed the paper, and headed for the front door of the Crow's Nest. The bell jangled in warning as the door slammed shut behind him.

Police Chief Carson was having his morning coffee and frowning over the *Scuttlebutt Weekly* when Ellery rapped sharply on his office doorframe.

Carson's frown only deepened at the sight of Ellery. He put down his blue coffee mug, laid aside the paper, and nodded at the chair in front of his cluttered desk.

"Can I help you, Mr. Page?"

"Can you?" Ellery retorted, taking the chair in front of Carson's desk. "Because it looks to me like my fate is sealed."

"Your fate is sealed?" Carson repeated thoughtfully. "That's a little dramatic."

"You read the paper. She's all but publicly accused me of murdering Trevor. If people didn't suspect me before, they sure will now."

"They did suspect you before."

Probably true, but not exactly conducive to defusing the situation.

"That's just great!" Ellery said hotly. "So that's it? I'm being tried in the court of public opinion before I'm even arrested?"

"Listen, before you get too bent out of—"

"Or am I about to be arrested? Should I call a lawyer?"

Carson let out a long, measured breath. "Ellery, will you calm the hell down?"

Hearing that quiet *Ellery* in Carson's deep voice had a funny and unexpected effect. Ellery's throat closed, choking off the rest of his words. He pressed his lips together, trying to look calm and controlled instead of as angry and upset and hurt as he really felt. Anger and upset were reasonable emotions given the circumstances, but hurt? Why? It's not like Carson had ever pretended to think he was anything but guilty.

It *was* hurtful, though. Hurtful that everyone in the village apparently believed he was capable of murder. Hurtful that Jack Carson had seemingly condoned this smear job disguised as a news article, because where else would Sue Lewis have got all these details?

Carson said, "Nothing has changed since yesterday. I don't have enough evidence to charge you. I have no plan to arrest you—at this time."

Ellery said tightly, "But I'm still a suspect."

"Yes. Of course you're still a suspect! Maples was killed in *your* shop with *your* sword after an argument with *you.* I'd be an idiot if I didn't consider you a suspect." Carson's tone did not soften, but he sounded less impatient as he added, "But you're not the only suspect. I did tell you that too."

"Sure, but I'm still the main suspect."

"Yes, you are." Carson studied him, said reluctantly, "Like I said yesterday, I don't know where Sue is getting her information, but it's not from me. I haven't spoken to her. Nor have I authorized anyone else in this office to communicate with the press."

Some of Ellery's fury faded. "Then where did she get all that about witnesses and my threatening Trevor? It's not even true!"

"If it's not true, then what are you worried about?"

"Because if it's in the newspaper, it looks true! How did she know that the murder weapon was a sword? Answer me that. We only figured it out yesterday afternoon."

The lines of Carson's face grew grimmer. "I have a theory."

"What's your theory?"

"I'm not sharing it with you. It's a personnel issue."

Ellery scowled but was silent. Carson had already said he had not spoken to Sue Lewis and that he did not have enough evidence to arrest Ellery. He had also conceded that there were other suspects.

He considered telling Carson about the spare key Aunt Eudora had given Dylan, but he remembered the alarm in Dylan's eyes, the clumsy lies. The more he thought about it, the more he believed Dylan had forgotten about that key until Ellery had reminded him, and that once he had remembered, he had been terrified. That didn't mean he hadn't killed Trevor, but if he had, the spare key hadn't figured into it. And honestly, Ellery just didn't believe Dylan had killed Trevor. Maybe he was being naive, but he felt sure that if Dylan were going to kill someone, it wouldn't be like that. It wouldn't be in a cold-blooded, premeditated way that threw suspicion on a friend.

"What?" Carson asked, jarring Ellery out of his thoughts.

"What?"

Carson's eyes were very bright, very keen. "You just thought of something."

"It's not important."

"How about you let me decide what's important?"

"It's a personnel issue," Ellery retorted.

Carson gave him a long, direct look from under his formidable eyebrows.

"Honestly, it's not important."

Ellery and Carson studied each other. Ellery found it suddenly difficult to look away.

He found himself wondering about that wedding band on Carson's left hand. He couldn't help thinking that if Carson was married to a man, he'd have heard about it. It was bound to be a point of local gossip in a small town like Pirate's Cove. It just would be. But he'd never heard a hint of anything like that.

And yet, he couldn't get over his conviction that Carson was gay.

Maybe closeted?

Or was it possible his orientation was even unacknowledged—unrecognized?—by Carson?

Except... It was that "Clear Vista" thing. Carson was not a man to dodge uncomfortable truths. His own or anyone else's.

And there was also the fact that Ellery's instincts for this kind of thing were far from infallible. He had been pretty sure when he met Dylan that Dylan was gay—to Dylan's huge amusement. So...

Carson glanced down at the newspaper lying on his ink blotter, glanced back at Ellery, said brusquely, "Is that it? Any other questions?"

Ellery said slowly, "Yes, I do have one more question."

"Which is?"

"Do you think I killed Trevor?"

Carson didn't hesitate. "It doesn't matter what I think. I have to follow the evidence. It'll be up to a court to weigh the merits of that evidence when the case finally goes to trial."

"I understand. I still want to know if you think I'm a murderer."

Carson looked suddenly weary. "I've been a cop for over a decade. One of the first lessons I learned is that good people do bad things and bad people do good things."

Why did it matter to him what Carson believed? But somehow it did.

"Sure, I believe that. But this wasn't an act committed in the heat of the moment. This would have been planned. It would have been…premeditated."

"*Cold-blooded* is the word you're looking for," Carson said.

"Okay, yes. Cold-blooded. Which I'm not. But also, if I'm the killer, really, *really* stupid. Why would I plan a crime where everything points to me as being guilty?"

"Maybe you are stupid."

Ellery reddened. After a moment, he shrugged and rose. "Maybe I am."

He headed for the door to Carson's office. As he reached for the handle, Carson said, "I don't think you're stupid. And…I don't think you killed Trevor Maples. But if enough evidence indicates otherwise, then it'll be my job to arrest you and allow the law to take its course."

Without turning, Ellery nodded, opened the door, and stepped into the bustling office. He closed the door quietly behind him.

CHAPTER TEN

He'd been wrong about one thing. Murder was good for business.

In fact, murder was *great* for business. That Monday the Crow's Nest made more money than it had in the last month. It seemed like everyone in Pirate's Cove had a sudden need for the latest release by Kate White or Lee Child or Agatha Christie.

No lie. Ellery actually had one flustered lookie-loo glance at a bookshelf and ask for whatever was new from Agatha Christie.

After Pandora Carter and the Out Damn Spot cleaning crew had finished up, there really wasn't much for the citizens of Pirate's Cove to gawk over besides a slight, irregular darkening, like the shadow of a rain cloud, in the center of the wooden floor. That didn't stop them from dropping in.

Nobody came right out and asked if he'd committed murder, but he was definitely being observed—there were even a few surreptitious photos taken on phones of him ringing up customers. He was asked how he was feeling, and how was business, and if he'd changed his mind about living in their little town, and if he'd read that morning's edition of the *Scuttlebutt Weekly*. He smiled blandly, answered vaguely, and kept ringing up all those lovely sales.

The security company showed up and quoted several discouragingly pricy options for alarm systems. Ellery looked over the quotes, promised to get back to the company with an answer, and paid for the shiny new locks on the front door.

On the one hand, it was nice to experience a profitable day. On the other hand, Scene of the Crime was probably not a sustainable business model.

The rush finally slowed about two, and Ellery felt comfortable digging out his sack lunch of tuna salad made with avocado, Greek yogurt, arugula and tomatoes on wheat bread. He made himself comfortable on the long wooden library bench against the far wall. He was eating his sandwich and watching the boats bobbing in the choppy waters of the harbor when Dylan rushed into the shop, closing the door and leaning against it as though being pursued by bloodhounds.

His silver hair was as close to disheveled as Ellery had seen it, and he looked wild-eyed, scanning the room until he spotted Ellery over on the bench, sandwich halfway to his mouth.

"You didn't tell him," Dylan gasped. "I was so sure you would. So *I* told him."

"Told who?" Ellery asked blankly. Whatever this was, it could not be good.

"Chief Carson." Dylan shoved the swoop of hair off his face and came toward Ellery, who made room on the bench. Dylan sat down, put his face in his hands. "I'm such a fool."

Appetite gone, Ellery dropped the rest of his sandwich in the paper bag. "What did you tell Chief Carson?"

"I told him about the spare key."

Ellery opened his mouth, then closed it.

Dylan gave him a sideways look. "I was positive you were going to tell him that Eudora had given me that key, so

I thought I better get in there as soon as possible to explain my position."

"What's your position?"

Dylan groaned. "I don't have one!"

Ellery suppressed a smile. It wasn't really funny—although, yeah, kind of.

Dylan looked at him. "Go ahead. Laugh. I deserve it. I just walked into his office, told Carson I knew it looked bad, and blurted the whole thing out."

"What did he say?"

"He said he had no idea what I was talking about, but that he could guess." Dylan's expression grew guilty. "The thing is, I fibbed. When they—the police—asked if I was aware of any extra keys to the Crow's Nest floating around, I said I wasn't. It was such a stupid lie. I'd forgotten Tommy would know. But I thought if I admitted I had a key, it would make me a suspect too. And unlike you, there really *was* bad blood between me and Trevor."

"Ah." So much for Ellery's ability to read people. He had been so sure Dylan had forgotten all about that key, but Dylan's shock had been due to the discovery that other people knew about it.

Still, he had been right about one thing. Dylan wasn't a murderer.

Or at least, he thought he was right about that. Dylan was still running around loose, so it seemed like Carson didn't think he was guilty either.

"And Carson knows you didn't do it. Despite what some people around here might say." Dylan's voice broke into Ellery's musings.

"What makes you think that?"

"He's not stupid, for one thing."

"Yeah, well. It's going to take more than that to keep me out of jail."

Dylan shook his head. "I don't know where Sue came up with all that stuff about you for the *Scuttlebutt*. I mean, we all know Trevor was annoying, but not slay-on-your-own-premises kind of annoying. Even *I* didn't need him gone that much."

"Someone did, that's for sure."

"Yes." Dylan's tone was thoughtful.

"Who do you think killed him?" Ellery asked curiously.

"Janet," Dylan said at once. "His ex-wife."

"But weren't they divorced a long time ago?"

"My dear fellow," Dylan said, "do you think in five years you'll be feeling more kindly toward Todd?"

"No," Ellery said flatly.

"Exactly. And you weren't married to Todd. He didn't cheat you out of your fair share of money and property."

"Okay, but still. It's a weird crime for a woman to commit. I don't know if Trevor was actually killed here. Maybe his body was moved here later. A woman couldn't do that. Not on her own."

"A bodybuilder could," Dylan inserted.

Ellery stared at him. "Are there any bodybuilder women in Pirate's Cove?"

Dylan looked abashed. "Not that I know of. No. Go ahead, you were saying?"

"I was saying, even if Trevor was killed here in my shop, it's hard to picture how it would happen. The killer would have to climb on something, probably the stepstool, to get the sword down. Even on the stool, most women wouldn't be tall enough to reach that high."

"Janet's tall. She's taller than me. She could reach it."

"Even so, can you imagine how that would have worked?"

"No, but I know Janet. She's not the forgiving kind. Not that I blame her in this case. Trevor was a swine. Talk about pirates." Dylan seemed to think that over. He said slowly, "And you know, now that I think of it, there is *something* going on with Janet. I'm sure of it."

"What do you mean?"

"She's a member of the Monday Night Scrabblers, which you're still welcome to join, by the way. It would do you a world of good to get out of that crypt once in a while. Have a few drinks, have a few laughs, make a few friends."

"I'm out of the crypt right now, if you'll notice."

"You know what I mean."

Yes. Ellery knew. He missed Scrabble. He missed hanging out with friends after work, having a few drinks, having a few laughs over games of wit and skill. Maybe if he'd made more effort to participate in village events, become part of the fabric of village life, everyone wouldn't now be so quick to assume his guilt.

He said, "Maybe once renovations on the house are done."

"Anyway, last Monday she canceled because she had a last-minute appointment at the beauty salon."

"So?"

Dylan held up a finger. "One, she never cancels. Janet is our Scrabble champion."

"Hm," Ellery said disapprovingly. *Champion?* That caught him on the quick. He *definitely* needed to make time for the Monday Night Scrabblers.

"Secondly, she was being very mysterious about the reason for the beauty appointment."

Ellery laughed. He'd been hoping Dylan was onto something, but this sounded pretty thin. "She had a date. So what?"

"Janet doesn't date."

"Okay, I give up."

Dylan held up a second finger, although his math was definitely off. "Janet doesn't date. Except once, when she and Trevor were toying with getting back together. And that romantic interlude ended when he got her to sign over her interest in Gimcrack Antiques."

"Ah-ha!" Ellery didn't know if it was really an *ah-ha!* moment, but Dylan seemed to expect a reaction.

Dylan sighed. "Why didn't you tell Chief Carson about the spare key?"

"Oh." Ellery made a face. "Because we're friends. And because I know you didn't kill anyone."

To his surprise, Dylan groaned. "I know you didn't kill Trevor either, but I still kept quiet to the police about that key." He threw an arm around Ellery's shoulders to give him a quick hug. "Thank you, Ellery. I won't forget this. You're a better friend than I am, Gunga Din."

* * * * *

The wind off the harbor was chilly when Ellery locked up at five.

Not that he really suspected Janet of slaying Trevor, but it couldn't hurt to ask a few questions. Carson had said to let him know if he could think of anything that would help establish his innocence, so okay. Surely, all he had to do was come up with enough reasonable doubt of his own guilt to encourage the police to look for a more viable victim. He would go right down his list of possible contenders, which, according to almost everyone he'd talked to, Janet's name should be heading.

He crossed the cobbled village square with its old-fashioned lampposts and urns of windblown flowers, turned down a narrow street. This was the newest part of the village; most of the tall brick buildings dating from the 1920s.

He couldn't help noticing that a few people crossed to the other side of the street when they spotted him, but whatever. That's what happened when you were front-page news. He was going to clear his name, and then they could all feel appropriately ashamed of themselves. Or not. But either way he'd have the satisfaction of proving them all wrong.

And then maybe he'd move back to New York, because by that point he'd doubtlessly be bankrupt.

When he reached Old Salt Stationery, he ducked inside, hoping to avoid curious gazes, but he needn't have worried. The shop was empty of customers.

Ellery looked around the small store. Boxes of notepads and note cards, calendars featuring Thomas Kincaid lighthouses and cute animals, high-end pens and bookmarks and magnets were neatly arranged by size and color on shelving units. One wall was devoted to greeting cards. The opposite wall was filled with rolls of colorful wrapping paper and ribbons. Three floral parasols hung from the ceiling. It was almost eerily tidy. As though an OCD Mary Poppins had organized every inch of space.

Ellery pinpointed Janet in her usual spot by the front counter, her bony nose stuck in a book titled *The Courage to Be Disliked*.

Janet glanced up, spied him, sniffed, and pushed her glasses back farther up her nose as she watched his approach. Ellery raised his hand in greeting and smiled ingratiatingly. He usually did very well with that smile—it had even won him two toothpaste commercials back when he'd been trying for a career in acting—but Janet wasn't having any. She wrinkled her nose as though catching a whiff of something nasty on the breeze.

Could she really have killed Trevor? Observing her now, it seemed more unlikely than ever, but where the heart was willing…

Not surprising that Janet and Trevor hadn't worked out. Trevor had been the kind of guy who wore a yachting cap and brass anchor buttons but hated sailing. His clothes had been expensive but never quite right. He had worn too much jewelry, too much aftershave, and laughed too loudly. He was especially unpleasant when he didn't get his way—so unpleasant, in fact, that he usually *did* get his way.

Janet, on the other hand, was tall, thin, pale as milk, and lank-haired. She looked like someone destined to be cast as New England spinster, schoolmarm, or witch burned on a bonfire.

People changed, of course, but it was really hard imagining what on earth could have originally drawn two such dissimilar types together.

"Hi, Mrs. Maples, how are you today?" Ellery kept smiling, and Janet kept staring like a zoologist confronted with an unknown species.

"Mr. Page?" If possible, she looked more disapproving. "Very well, thank you. How are *you*?" It was pointed. "I saw your picture in the social column this morning."

She had never struck him as having a sense of humor, so maybe she was being ironic.

"Sadly, they failed to capture my good side," Ellery said.

She sniffed again.

He refused to be daunted. "Anyway, that's why I'm here. I wanted to tell you I'm sorry about what happened to Trevor, and to personally assure you I had absolutely nothing to do with his death."

"If you had nothing to do with his death, why are you sorry?" she asked coolly.

"I'm s…what?"

Janet repeated, "If you had nothing to do with my ex-husband's death, I'm not sure why you're here expressing regret. I'm further confused as to why you're expressing regret to *me*. My relationship with Trevor ended years ago."

"I guess because the paper basically accused me of murder, and I wanted to make it clear to everyone that that's a lie. I knew you were once married, and I assumed you probably had mixed emotions about his passing."

"Mixed emotions? Not really. My feelings have always been perfectly clear-cut where Trevor was concerned."

Ellery had a flash of inspiration. "He always spoke highly of you t—"

"Ha! You're clearly thinking of someone else," she said crisply. "The only person Trevor ever had a kind word for was Logan."

"Logan?"

"His brother." Her smile was sardonic. "And here I thought you two were such good friends."

This was not going at all according to plan. "I wouldn't say *that*."

"I wouldn't either."

"Okaaay. Again, sorry for your loss. Such as it was. And you can rest assured, I wasn't involved."

"I don't care if you were involved or not. Trevor has been no concern of mine for a very long time."

"Right. Well…" Ellery began to retreat. There was something unnerving about her.

"We reap what we sow," Janet said almost cheerily. "When you're my age, you'll understand how true that is."

Ellery stopped retreating. "It sounds like you might have a couple of theories on who might have killed Trevor."

"I assume you did."

"I certainly did not. I just said I didn't."

Her mouth curved primly. "Just goes to show you can't believe everything you read in the papers."

What the... Janet Maples was definitely an odd duck. He was trying to think of an answer when she added, "Either way, all's well that ends well. Don't worry about unloading the Crow's Nest. I'll make you a very fair offer."

"I don't want a very fair offer. I don't plan on selling."

"That's brave, but you're not a businessman. You're an actor, aren't you? You must be eager to get back to the bright lights of Broadway."

"I'm not an actor. I'm a screenwriter. According to my agent, anyway. In the meantime, I'm a bookseller."

"I doubt that. But you've put a lot of work into the old place. I'll make you a very fair offer. Much fairer than Trevor would have."

The penny dropped. Ellery said, "Do you inherit Trevor's properties?"

"Of course."

Of course? Was that usual in a divorce? Didn't people change their wills after a divorce? Especially such a bitter divorce?

"I see," Ellery said. "I appreciate the offer, whatever it would have been, but the Crow's Nest is not for sale."

"Pride goeth before a fall," Janet said.

"What's that supposed to mean?"

"It's no secret you're struggling to keep your head above water. You're going to need cash pretty quick, according to scuttlebutt. Legal fees can mount up fast, take it from one who knows."

"All the same," Ellery said.

"Let me know if you change your mind," Janet said. "I'm guessing you will. And soon."

CHAPTER ELEVEN

No cars or motorbikes were allowed in the village center, so when Ellery left Old Salt Stationery, he had to walk back to the Crow's Nest to retrieve the VW. When he reached the bookshop, he spotted someone peering through the windows, hands cupped around her face. He felt a flash of unease, but then recognized Nora Sweeny.

Once upon a time, Nora had run the Pirate Cove Historical Society, but the building that had housed the society had been condemned and the land sold to, guess who? Trevor Maples. Trevor had built a bicycle rental shop on the property, which reportedly did a nice summer trade, but was closed during the winter months. As for the historical society, without a roof over its head, the organization had simply faded away like the town history it had hoped to preserve.

Nora was small, but her personality was mighty. She was slight as a child and stood just over five feet in her sensible shoes. Her eyes were gray and piercing. Her long iron-hued hair was worn in a tight ponytail. She was a little nosy and a little on the garrulous side, but Ellery liked her. She was sharp and lively and, for her age, surprisingly—or maybe it wasn't surprising, considering her age—unshockable. Even so, it had been a long day, and he was looking forward to going home and having a leisurely, hot bath and possibly a glass or two—or maybe a bottle—of wine.

"Hi, Nora! Did you need something?" he called.

Nora jumped guiltily. "Ellery! There you are. I thought you'd left for the day."

"I have. But I had to come back for my car."

Nora looked a bit confused but smiled anyway. "I wondered if you could spare a moment, dearie." She was the only person outside of a character in a play Ellery had ever heard use the term *dearie*.

He groaned inwardly, but said, "Sure. What's on your mind?"

"It's a little delicate; maybe we should step inside?" Nora suggested hopefully.

"If you'd prefer that." Ellery swallowed his sigh, unlocked the front door, and ushered her in.

Her gaze went instantly and unerringly to the darker patch in the center of the floor, and Ellery hoped this visit wasn't about Nora wanting a personal tour of the crime scene.

She met his gaze, and maybe she read what he was thinking because she said briskly, "First of all, I wanted to tell you how appalled I was by the story in the *Scuttlebutt*. Such an irresponsible thing for Sue Lewis to have done."

"Thank you," Ellery said.

"And I'm not the only person in the village who thinks so."

"I hope not. I guess people would rather believe an outsider killed Trevor than one of their own."

Nora said tartly, "I don't think most people give a hoot about Trevor Maples. Maybe you never noticed, but he wasn't well liked in Pirate's Cove. Nor are you an outsider. In fact, Trevor was more of an outsider than you. There have been Pages in Pirate's Cove since they first broke ground in the village."

Maybe so, and he appreciated what she was saying, but even if Ellery's distant family had lived in Pirate's Cove, most people did regard him as a stranger. He *was* a stranger. The feeling was mutual.

Nora was still running on. "This will all blow over. You'll see. Chief Carson is a very clever man. You might not think it to look at him, but he is. He has a way of ferreting out the truth. He's the one who figured out Elinor Christmas was stealing from the church fund, and that was practically the perfect crime."

Ellery grinned at both the "you might not think it to look at him," and the idea of Carson applying his master detective skills to pilfering from the collection box. "That's reassuring."

"It is. He's a very good man. A little gruff, but he's had his share of sorrow."

"Has he?" Ellery was unwillingly curious.

"Oh yes. His wife died, you know. They were childhood sweethearts. She was killed in a hit-and-run."

"*Here?*" He was genuinely shocked. Also surprised because cars weren't allowed in so much of the village—and the people who did drive, did so like they were afraid of getting their tires dirty.

"Oh no!" Nora looked equally shocked. "Not *here*. Heavens. In Los Angeles. Chief Carson moved to Pirate's Cove after his wife's death."

"I thought he grew up here."

Nora laughed at the idea. "Chief Carson? Oh no. He's from California. He was a homicide detective with LAPD. He wanted a change of pace, and I guess he got it."

"How long has he been chief of police?"

"It's been about five years now."

"I had no idea." To put it mildly. In fact, practically everything he had thought about Jack Carson was incorrect. He was straight, he was not an inexperienced small-town cop, and he was not a hometown hero. This was not even his hometown.

Nora squeezed his arm with her small, bony hand. "You see? You just have to have faith, hang tight, and this whole mess will all be sorted out."

"Thank you," Ellery said. He meant it. He didn't *believe* it. But he was still grateful to her for trying to reassure him.

"Now the other thing I wanted to talk to you about is the bookshop."

"What about it?" Surely Nora wasn't also going to offer to buy the Crow's Nest?

"I've been doing some thinking. I hope you won't take this the wrong way, but it's pretty obvious you really don't know very much about mysteries and crime novels."

"I'm learning," Ellery protested. "It's not my background, no, but I'm picking it up. At least I know Agatha Christie is dead."

"And that's a starting point," Nora said in the tone of a kindergarten teacher encouraging a backward toddler. "But it's also useful to keep track of who's still alive. For example, who wrote the Commissario Guido Brunetti series? Can you take a guess?"

"Professor Plum in the study with a poker?"

Nora laughed. "No. Donna Leon. What about the Dave Brandstetter series?"

"I'm guessing *not* Donna Leon?"

"And you're correct. Joseph Hansen wrote the Brand-stetter books."

Ellery said, "Okay, well, now I know more than I did this morning. So that's great. Thank you." He was hoping Nora would wind things up pretty quickly because he was already well aware he did not know a whole heck of a lot about the mystery genre—but he sure knew more than he had three months ago.

As if she read his thoughts, Nora's cheeks grew pink. She took a little breath as though bracing herself to take a punch. "What I was thinking was perhaps you'd like to hire me to work in the Crow's Nest with you."

Funny thing, his immediate reaction was *yes*! Then reality set in.

He said regretfully, "I wish I could, Nora, but I can't afford to hire anyone right now. Sue Lewis was right about one thing. The bookshop is failing."

"Oh, you don't have to pay me," Nora said quickly. "Not right away, at least. If the bookstore begins to turn a profit, it would be nice to earn a little extra money, but I'm all right, financially speaking. I have my late husband's social security as well as my own, and I have a small retirement fund. It's not that I *need* a job. I'd just like a job. And I think I'd be very well suited to working here. And you do, *desperately*, need help."

"Well, I don't think it's *that* desperate—"

"Oh, but it is," Nora said kindly but ruthlessly. "You're really very much out of your depth."

Ellery opened his mouth to object, and Nora said, "What's the hottest trend in cozy mystery?"

"Murder."

Nora blinked. "Magic, dearie. Witches, in particular."

"My second guess."

She smiled tentatively. "Now you're teasing me."

"Yes," Ellery said, though he was not. What he was doing was seriously considering her proposal. He did need help. Maybe not *desperately*, but as things stood, he couldn't step out for a sandwich or even use the restroom without risking losing a sale—and he couldn't afford to lose any sales. "What would you be getting out of this arrangement, though?"

"You can't imagine." She actually teared up. "It would be so lovely to have somewhere to go every day where I'm truly needed and can even make a contribution. Ever since the historical society closed..." She wiped her eyes. "You're too young to understand, but once you get to be a certain age, people treat you like you're on your way out. As though a lifetime of experience and knowledge means nothing. As though your just still *being* there irritates them. And you're such a lovely young man. So polite and kind."

"You're making me sound like Trevor's murderer for sure."

Nora gave a damp chortle. "You even have a sense of humor."

Ellery weighed the pros and cons, and it did seem like there were a lot more pros than cons.

"Are you sure you want to be so closely associated with me? Plenty of people—maybe your friends and neighbors—believe what Sue Lewis wrote."

"Anyone silly enough to make their minds up before they've heard the whole story isn't someone whose opinion matters to me."

Still Ellery hesitated. "Even if I don't get arrested, the shop may still go under. You might never get paid anything."

Nora said with touching solemnity, "If you let me work here, that will be all the pay I need. That's the truth."

"You're sure about that?"

"One hundred percent."

Convinced at last, Ellery smiled. "All right, then. You're hired. When can you start?"

He was startled when she gave him a blazing smile and threw her arms around him. "I'll be here at seven tomorrow!"

"Uh, I'll be here at eight," Ellery said. "See you then!"

* * * * *

The dog was sitting in the middle of the road.

On his way home from the bookshop, Ellery was listening to Ashley Serena (probably not the wisest choice for that dark, lonely drive) when The VW's headlights picked out the gleam of eyes first, and then Ellery saw the dark outline of a small animal—a dog—and hit the brakes.

The VW skidded across the highway, narrowly missing the dog, which sprang away. Ellery fought for control as the beetle started to spin, managing to straighten out before he went careening off the road. The car bumped onto the dirt shoulder, traveled forward, and came to a stop nosed into a leafy wall of tall hedge.

The CD player cut off, the engine died, the headlights went out. For a moment, Ellery sat motionless, breathing fast, shaking with adrenaline and relief.

Jesus Christ.

When he could think again, he turned the key in the ignition. Something clicked. That was all. The engine did not turn over. The car did not kick back to life. If anything, the surrounding silence seemed to deepen. He could hear the leaves of the hedge scraping against the front of the VW.

He dug his cell phone out, pressed the Home button, and saw an unsurprising absence of bars. No service.

Of course not. Because he was sitting on the edge of the flipping world, with nothing beneath him but a bottomless abyss of futility and failure.

Okay. Maybe not that bad.

But now what?

After a moment, he turned everything off, pushed the driver's door open, climbed out. The night air was cold and damp on his perspiring face. He shivered.

He thought he could see the faraway gleam of lights through the hedge. Maybe there was a house within walking distance.

The hedge rustled noisily next to him, and he jumped aside, expecting the next dire event: a bear, a serial killer, a—

A small black something pushed out of the wall of leaves and wriggled up to him, whining. The dog. No, it was a puppy.

"Hey, what are you doing out here?" Ellery knelt, and the puppy threw itself into his arms. It was too dark to really see, but he held a bundle of silky fur, floppy ears, wet, snuffling nose, and a frantically waving tail. The puppy's whimpers sounded nearly hysterical. Ellery knew the feeling.

He felt over the small, wiggling body, but the puppy did not appear to have a collar.

"How did you get here?"

The dog, naturally, had no answer.

Ellery scooped it up, holding it under his arm as he tried to peer through the hedge.

Yes. There was a house. It sat on a small hill, and lights burned cheerfully on the upstairs and downstairs levels.

He tucked the puppy more comfortably under his arm and walked along the hedge, seeking an opening. The puppy, seeking warmth, burrowed under his jacket, snuggling against his ribs.

It took a while, and he had to walk out of his way, but eventually Ellery found a small wrought-iron gate cut into the hedge. The gate was padlocked, but he put the puppy through the bars, vaulted over, picked the pup up, and walked on toward the house. Before long he reached the bottom of a short drive. A metal mailbox stood to the side, stenciled with lettering that read MAPLES.

It probably shocked him more than it should have. He was vaguely aware that Trevor had, like himself, lived outside the village proper.

So much for that idea. He really didn't have a lot of options, but for a few seconds, he stood there, trying to decide whether to proceed. All those blazing lights seemed to indicate someone was home. A housekeeper? A tenant? Maybe there was a girlfriend or a second wife? He'd never heard any mention of one, but it wasn't like he'd paid a lot of attention to Trevor's personal life. If anything, he'd tried to avoid hearing about Trevor.

Anyway, whoever was residing there would hopefully allow him to use the phone so he could call Robertson's Garage for a tow truck. He started up the drive toward the house.

The puppy now slept inside his partially zipped jacket. That warm, breathing weight snuggled against his body was comforting. The night was unnervingly dark, unnervingly quiet, and the sky was brilliant with stars that looked as cold and hard as ice chips. There was no other house for as far as he could see.

As he drew near, he could see the house was large and modern in design. It looked a bit like a small prison but with lots of large windows. Maybe one of those more progressive institutions.

He went up the cement walk, rang the doorbell, and waited.

Nothing happened.

He stepped back, studying the lighted windows, and tried buzzing the bell again. He could hear the ring, a brisk, businesslike zap of sound echoing through the house.

The blinds didn't budge, the drapes didn't twitch, no one called out, and no one came to answer the door.

Maybe the lights were on a timer. Ellery left his lights on a timer so he didn't have to stumble around in the dark on the nights he arrived home late, which was most nights.

For laughs, he tried the front-door handle. It was locked. OF COURSE.

He wondered if the police had already searched Trevor's home. He was pretty sure that searching a victim's home was standard procedure for New York City police, but this was Pirate's Cove. Was it possible the house hadn't been searched yet? Nah. That was wishful thinking. Carson's people would have been through the house first thing Sunday morning. Or would it be the job of the state police? Too bad he wasn't more up on his mystery reading because he'd probably have a better idea. As it was, he just didn't know.

What he *did* know was it was cold, it was late, and he did not want to walk the three miles back to town.

He also couldn't help thinking that if the house hadn't been searched yet, this was a once-in-a-lifetime opportunity.

In fact, even if the house *had* been searched, this was a once-in-a-lifetime opportunity. Because even without knowing what he might be looking for, going through Trevor's home was going to tell him a lot about Trevor, and the more he knew about Trevor, the better his chances of figuring out who was most likely to want him out of the way.

A murder investigation always began with the victim. After three months of owning a mystery bookshop, that much he did know.

Still, he did not want—could not afford—to be arrested for breaking and entering, especially breaking and entering his supposed victim's property. Sue Lewis would have a field day with that.

There was probably an alarm system.

Even as Ellery reminded himself of these things, he was walking along the side of the house, looking for another way in. Maybe an unlatched side door. Maybe an open window. Maybe—

He stopped in his tracks, staring in disbelief. Was he dreaming? It couldn't be true.

But yes, it was true. A ground-floor window had been left a couple of inches open. The night breeze gently stirred the draperies.

If he could just shimmy it a bit, he might be able to raise it enough to get through.

Puppy sleeping at his feet in the damp grass, Ellery spent the next five minutes gently wiggling and pushing the window until he could create a gap wide enough to climb inside. With one leg hooked into the sill, he hoisted himself up and dropped into the dark room.

He felt his way around the room until he located a light switch. He flipped the switch and saw he was in a dining room. He set the puppy on the oval dining table, where it blinked sleepily at him and then curled into a small black ball, nose tucked beneath its tail.

His heart was thumping unpleasantly in his chest. It wasn't just the fear of being caught, though that was intense; it was also the sick feeling of knowing he was crossing lines that decent people did not cross. He didn't want to go to prison for something he hadn't done. But how many crimes was he prepared to commit in order to avoid that fate?

He wasn't sure. And the truth was, as much as he didn't like what he was doing, he wasn't prepared to turn back either. Instead, he left the dining room and wandered into the adjoining living room.

The first thing he noticed was that there were indeed timers set up to turn on the lights. The second thing he noticed was that the living room was a large, airy space with sharply vaulted ceilings and a natural-stone fireplace. The room had the sterile look of professional decorator left to their own devices, but there were a few old family photos on the fireplace, including a wedding photograph of Trevor and Janet. Ellery studied it curiously. They both looked a lot younger and a lot happier, but even back then they had not looked like people who belonged together. Not a matched pair.

Not that that meant much. Their friends used to say he and Todd had looked like a couple in a magazine. Ellery had been thinking *GQ*, but *National Enquirer* had been closer to the truth.

Still, the pictures offered unexpected insight into Trevor. Ellery would never have thought him capable of sentimentality, but the photos told a different story.

Unless they were intended for someone else's benefit?

A door to the right of the living room caught Ellery's eye, and, heart thumping noisily, he gently pushed it open, feeling again for a light switch.

When the overhead light blazed on, he saw that he was in a study or office. A desktop computer sat on a suspiciously empty desk. A low bookshelf contained several volumes on real estate, antiques collecting, and investment banking.

He crossed the room to the desk, uncomfortably aware that, with the blinds raised and the lights on, this room probably looked like a tiny movie set from a mile away.

Though what anyone would be doing standing in the dark countryside watching this house, he couldn't imagine.

He opened the top desk drawer and was startled to see a bundle of papers sitting there for anyone to find, positioned as neatly and conveniently as a stage prop. Printed across the top of the first page were the words *Last Will and Testament of Trevor Maples*.

"You're kidding," Ellery murmured. He pulled the document out and skimmed the pages, skipping the boring passages of legalese, until he came to the meat of the behests. His eyes widened in astonishment as he read that Trevor had left almost all his worldly belongings—and there seemed to be a lot of them—to a Logan Maples.

Who was Logan Maples? Where had he heard that name before?

It came to him. That very afternoon in Old Salt Stationery. Janet had said the only person Trevor ever had a kind word for was his brother, Logan. Well, clearly he'd had more than a kind word for him.

This news was going to come as a shock to Janet, that was for sure.

He began to refold the thick document, when someone or something banged against the front door of the house. Ellery gasped, dropped the will, snatched it up again, and thrust it back into the drawer, easing it closed. His heart was in overdrive.

The police!

Wait. No. The police would identify themselves. There would be sirens, there would be flashing lights, there would be the crackle of radios. At the very least there would be voices. Voices yelling, *Open up! Police!*

There was none of that.

Just that angry pounding on the front door.

Who—or what—was *that*?

Moot point. He needed to get out of the house pronto.

He started for the study window and then remembered the puppy he had left sleeping on the dining-room table.

Oh no. Oh, for God's sake. But he couldn't just leave it. For one thing, the dog made it as plain as a neon sign that someone had broken in, and the most cursory dusting for fingerprints would reveal who the intruder was. For another...

Well, he couldn't just leave it, that was all. Not after traipsing cross-country with the little beast cuddled against his heart.

Ellery snapped out the overhead light, crept down the hall, and paused, listening. The banging had stopped. The puppy was whimpering with increasing volume. Any second now he'd start yapping for sure.

He bit his lip, trying to decide what to do. Really, what *could* he do? His options were limited. He dropped down on the floor, crawled across the living room, staying beneath the sightlines of the windows, until he reached the dining room, where the puppy was now yipping, expressing his distress more forcefully, as puppies are wont to do.

"*Shhh. Shhh,*" Ellery hissed. "I'm right here."

He reached up and snapped off the dining-room light, then felt his way across the room to the table. He scooped up the puppy, who greeted him with frantic kisses and almost human sounds of complaint, and shoved the squirming bundle into his jacket. He made his way to the open window.

All the while, Ellery was thinking about fingerprints, and why someone would knock on a dead man's door, and whether this could possibly be a trap. But again, if the police were banging on the front door, they'd identify themselves.

And if it *wasn't* the police...

Yikes. No. Much better to avoid any confrontation.

Quickly and quietly, Ellery climbed out the dining-room window and dropped down to the grass below. He picked himself up and turned to run, but curiosity stopped him. He leaned back against the side of the house, listening. He could hear someone moving around the front yard, crashing through the flower beds.

Ellery tiptoed around the building, stepping cautiously, trying his best not to make a sound. The puppy was licking his chin. "Go to sleep," he whispered, backing along the side of the house. He could feel the pup staring up at him, and he prayed it wouldn't start whimpering again.

He reached the end of the house, craned his head around the corner, and was startled to see Janet Maples a few feet away, peering through one of the front windows. She was holding what appeared to be a crowbar.

He ducked back, heart jumping around in his chest.

He risked another look and saw Janet testing the window to see if it was locked.

Great minds.

If Janet was looking for what he thought she was, she was in for a rude awakening.

If she found the will, would she destroy it? That would be a drastic step. Then again, so was breaking and entering. But how likely was it that copy was the only one? Maybe it wasn't even the final draft. He didn't remember noticing whether it was signed or not. He had been so startled to see Trevor's brother's name as primary beneficiary.

Ellery withdrew the way he had come, soundlessly backtracking the length of the house. When he reached the end of the building, he turned and sprinted down the grassy hill, bypassing the driveway and heading straight for the tall line of hedge hiding his car from sight.

With every step, he expected to hear Janet shouting after him, but the crisp, cold night remained silent but for the pound of his feet and the huffs of his frosty breath.

He jumped over the little gate, hiked down the road until he reached his VW, gleaming and motionless in the moonlight. He half climbed, half fell inside, deposited the puppy on the passenger seat, and tried the engine again.

Sometimes when it stalled out—

Yes!

To his abject relief, the VW sputtered noisily into life.

"Halle-freaking-lujah," Ellery muttered, shifting into gear. The VW rolled gently off the dirt shoulder and bumped back onto the highway.

Ellery continued to putt-putt along for a few yards, and then he turned his headlights on, hit the gas, and sped away toward home.

CHAPTER TWELVE

"I get that, Cyrus, but I can't arrest her for murder without more to go on than they used to go out."

Police Chief Carson was on the phone when Ellery was ushered into his office the next morning. The chief's gaze was not particularly welcoming, but he nodded for Ellery to take the chair in front of his desk.

Ellery sat down and stared out the window. He tried to look like he was not listening to every word, but of course he was. He was also uncomfortably aware that Carson smelled like he had just stepped out of the shower and that his eyes were the same blue-green as the sun-dazzled water in the harbor—uncomfortable because now he knew Carson was not only straight, but had a tragic past.

"I don't disbelieve you, but I'm not investigating her real-estate business." Carson sounded patient but weary.

Ellery risked a peek, and he thought the chief looked like he had not been sleeping well. There were little lines around his eyes.

There was a prolonged silence while the chief listened and Cyrus talked.

Carson shifted in his chair, caught Ellery's gaze, and his mouth curved in the briefest of rueful smiles. His eyes rose heavenward. Ellery bit back a grin.

At last, Carson said mildly, "I'm not forgetting who my friends are. You've been very supportive. You can rely on my vote."

He replaced the phone in its cradle and sighed.

Ellery said, "The mayor believes Thomasina Rider killed Trevor Maples?"

Carson tilted his head, considering Ellery. "You know what they say about eavesdroppers?"

"I know if you were worried about me eavesdropping, you wouldn't have had me shown into your office while you were on the phone." Ellery added, "You wanted me to see that there *are* other suspects."

"Very good." Carson sat back in his chair. "Okay, to what do I owe this visit?"

"Well…" This was both awkward and tricky. Ellery's instinct was to keep quiet about his previous night's adventures, but Janet's behavior was sufficiently alarming that the chief surely needed to know about it.

Also, he was worried about his fingerprints showing up in a subsequent search of Trevor's home. It might be best to get out ahead of that potential discovery.

"Well?" Carson prompted.

"I was driving home last night, and I almost hit a dog. Actually, it was a puppy."

"You did or you didn't hit the dog?"

"I didn't hit it."

"Okay. So?"

"But in trying to avoid hitting it, I went off the road, and then I couldn't get my car to start."

"Are you reporting a traffic accident? Because I have—"

"No." Ellery drew in a breath. "No. I'm just… This is awkward."

Carson said dryly, "You should be used to awkward by now."

"No kidding." Ellery straightened, hands braced on his knees. "Okay, here's the thing. I couldn't get my car to start, and I couldn't get a signal on my phone, so I thought I would go for help. I saw some lights through a hedge, and I started walking. Well, it turned out the house was Trevor's."

The room was suddenly, unnervingly still.

"I didn't know it was Trevor's house until I saw the mailbox."

"Go on."

"There were a bunch of lights on, so I thought maybe he had a housekeeper or a tenant or someone else staying there." Ellery did not like the expression on Carson's face. "You know, I didn't know anything about Trevor before all this happened."

Carson said, "I hope to God you're not going to tell me what I think you're going to tell me."

The combination of Carson's very quiet voice and bleak expression caused Ellery's nerve to fail. He blurted, "I walked up to the house and saw Janet Maples skulking around the front with a crowbar. So I turned and left. When I got back to my car, it started, so I drove home. That's it."

After a moment, Carson said, "That's *it*?"

"Yes. That's it. I thought you should know."

Carson's eyes narrowed. "You didn't go inside the house? You didn't remove anything from inside the house?"

"Remove anything? No. Was something removed?"

"I'll ask the questions. Did you go inside the house?"

"No." Ellery bit his lip.

"Are you lying to me?"

"Yes." Ellery dropped his face in his hands. He said muffledly, "Yes, I went inside. But I didn't— I'm telling you the truth about everything else. Janet was there with a crowbar. And I didn't take anything from the house."

"Nothing at all?"

"*Nothing.* I swear it."

"You didn't take papers from the desk in Trevor's office?"

"No. Of course not."

Carson looked unimpressed. "What about a small canine that was apparently walking up and down the dining-room table?"

Ellery gulped. "Oh. Right. I did take the puppy. But I brought the puppy, so that doesn't count."

Carson repeated slowly, "You brought a puppy to your B&E."

Ellery sat bolt upright, eyes wide. "It wasn't a burglary. It was exactly what I told you. Except, yes, I did go in the house."

Carson said—and he seemed sincerely appalled, "*Why?* Why in God's name would you do that? You're already the main suspect—"

"That's why! I thought if I had a little insight into Trevor, it would help me figure out who might have wanted him out of the way."

"That's not your job! That's *my* job!"

"I know, but you said if the evidence was there, you'd be happy to arrest me."

"I didn't say I would be *happy*. I said—" Carson broke off. "Do you have any idea—" He cut that off too. He shook his head. "I can't believe this. I can't believe anyone would be this...this..."

"Dumb," agreed Ellery. "I know. Me neither."

"Yeah, but you're not dumb. That's what I don't get. Why would you do something so reckless?"

"It didn't seem reckless at the time. It seemed like an opportunity."

"To get yourself thrown in prison, certainly." Despite his words, Carson seemed to be cooling down fast, his thoughts running in another direction.

"Is the will missing?" Ellery asked. "Is that what happened? Janet took the will?"

Carson stared at him. "You saw the will?"

"Yes. I saw that Trevor left everything to his brother. That was why, when I saw Janet lurking last night, I felt like I needed to tell you. Because if she thought she was inheriting Trevor's empire, that gives her a motive." He admitted, "Otherwise I would have kept quiet."

Carson rubbed his forehead like he felt a headache coming on.

"Was it a trap?"

"Was what a trap?"

"Was the will left there to lure someone into stealing it?"

"No."

"But then how did you know—"

"One of Trevor's neighbors reported Mrs. Maples's car parked at the bottom of the road. This morning I drove over to see what she'd been up to."

"I didn't think Trevor had neighbors. It was so dark out there." Ellery considered. "If Janet stole the will…"

"That wasn't the only copy of the will. Logan Maples also has a copy, as does Trevor's lawyer. I don't know why Janet Maples imagined taking the will would be useful."

"It was probably a bad impulse," Ellery said.

"You'd know about that." Carson was silent, thinking. "Was that it? Anything else you want to confess?"

Ellery shook his head.

"Then listen—and listen carefully. Do not tell anyone about last night. Do you understand?"

Ellery nodded.

"Do not let anyone know that you saw Trevor's will or that you have any idea as to its contents. Clear?"

"Yes."

"Also, stay away from Janet Maples. Don't confront her. Don't question her. Don't even wish her a good morning should your paths cross."

"Okay, come on. I can't—"

"Got it?"

"Got it."

"One last thing. No more playing detective."

"I wasn't. I just thought if I—"

"No more thinking."

Ellery started to respond irritably and then caught what could have been the faintest glimmer of…what? Not sympathy. Not amusement. Not an easily identified emotion in Jack's—Chief Carson's—eyes.

"Leave the police work to the police," Carson warned. "I know from your perspective this is excruciating, but that's how it works. It's not like the books you sell. A homicide investigation takes time. And that's a good thing because it's important to get it right."

Ellery sighed. Nodded. "Okay."

"Now out." Carson pointed at the door. "I've got work to do." He opened the file on the desk in front of him.

* * * * *

"He doesn't have a microchip," Dr. Vincent informed Ellery when he stopped by the vet's office to pay for the puppy's examination. "He hasn't been neutered yet, and I'm guessing he hasn't had any of his shots. He's underweight, and we're testing for parasites, but otherwise he gets a clean bill of health."

"That's good, I guess. Do you think maybe he belonged to Trevor Maples?"

"Trevor Maples? No. He didn't like dogs. He had a cat at one time, but she ran away."

And who could blame her?

Ellery said, "Will you run an ad in the paper to try and locate whoever lost him?"

Dr. Vincent said, "We can try that, but I don't think he's a runaway. I think someone dumped him."

"Dumped him?"

"It happens more often than we'd like to think. Some people have the mistaken idea that domestic dogs can survive just fine in the wild, but it's not true. And this little guy is only about four months old. He wouldn't survive for long, in any case." Vincent was tall and thin with a receding hairline and mournful brown eyes behind round spectacles. "He's a cutie. You sure you want to put him up for adoption?"

"He's so little, and I'm never home." Ellery liked dogs, but he really wasn't in a position to look after a puppy. He wasn't sure he could support himself much longer, so taking on another mouth to feed was a bad idea.

"He's already started to bond with you."

They watched the puppy nibble on Ellery's fingers. Ellery winced, but that was not the puppy's sharp teeth so much as the idea of giving the little monster away. This was what came of letting a dog sleep in the bed with you, but it was so cold in the mausoleum of Captain's Seat.

Cold and drafty. And lonely.

He hadn't been able to hold out against the puppy's whimpers.

Ellery shook his head. "It wouldn't be fair to him."

As though he understood, the puppy stopped nibbling, sat up, and howled.

Ellery and Dr. Vincent exchanged startled looks.

"I think he disagrees," Dr. Vincent said. "But it's your call."

Reluctantly, Ellery gave another shake of his head. He bent, kissed the puppy's little smooshed monkey face, and gave him a final pat. "Good luck, little buddy." He was surprised and a bit embarrassed at the way his throat closed up.

The puppy was still howling when the glass door shut behind Ellery.

CHAPTER THIRTEEN

"**S**ue Lewis didn't like that," Nora said with satisfaction.

After he'd got back from the vet's, Ellery had asked Nora to call the *Scuttlebutt Weekly* to come get their papers. No way was he giving Sue Lewis even one inch of real estate within his bookshop. Not anymore. Not when Sue's editorial that morning had been Sue musing in print as to why PICO PD seemed afraid to make an arrest in the Trevor Maples case when it was perfectly clear to everyone in town who the perpetrator was.

"I don't know what her problem is," Ellery said. "But if she thinks I'm going to contribute to her business while she destroys mine, she's mistaken."

Nora said, "Her campaign probably isn't as personal as it feels. This is likely more about Chief Carson than you."

"I don't see how that can be true. She barely mentions him. It's all about me and how I'm a menace to society."

Nora smiled knowingly. "Sue's had her nose out of joint about Chief Carson for a long time. It was one thing when he first moved here. He was recently widowed, and no one expected him to take a romantic interest. In fact, he and Sue started a friendship. They'd have dinner once in a while or meet for lunch. We all wondered if it might turn into something more in time—and it was pretty clear Sue hoped it would turn into something more—but it never did. No more than it did for any of the other ladies in this town who figure five years is a long enough mourning period for any man."

"I see," Ellery said, inexplicably cheered by the idea of Chief Carson in a permanent state of mourning. "But even so."

"For the last year, Sue's been using her editorial column to vague-post her dissatisfaction with the police department on everything from coming down too hard on inebriated tourists to being too soft on local delinquents. She never mentions the chief directly, but it's pretty obvious where she thinks the blame lies."

"Yikes." Ellery was grinning at Nora's vague-post comment. Nora was a real character, and he was starting to think hiring her had been one of his best decisions yet. Not only did she know about a million times more than he did about the mystery and crime genre, she was like a walking encyclopedia when it came to the village. Plus, it was just really nice having someone to talk to during the day.

The bell on the door rang at that moment, and a young woman popped in with one child in a stroller and another clutching her hand. A tourist, clearly, because after yesterday's rush—and this morning's editorial—none of the locals were dropping by.

Nora took charge of the young woman, quickly determining that her interest was more toward psychological suspense than cozy, and Ellery went back to sorting through a box of old paperbacks he'd lugged up from the cellar.

In a short while, the young woman left with three paperbacks and a hardcover copy of the first book in the Chet Gecko series.

"That went well." Nora was beaming.

"We just need another nineteen customers like her this afternoon," Ellery agreed.

Nora made a *pshaw* sound, but her attention was elsewhere. She studied the flyer Tommy Rider had left with Ellery on Saturday. She shook her head.

"What?" Ellery asked.

"When thieves fall out."

"Very cryptic."

Nora's smile was sour. "She's a pretty girl. You can't argue with that."

"Do you think she'll be the next mayor of Pirate's Cove?"

"No." Nora had no hesitation. "Never. Thomasina is smart, very smart, and very ambitious, but she's too decorative. Wives won't vote for her."

"That's a little sexist."

"Just because it's sexist doesn't mean it's not true." Nora added, "Besides, Cyrus is a perfectly good mayor. He understands that while everyone wishes business was better and we were all making more money, no one wants to lose our island way of life. Neither Thomasina nor Trevor grasped that. All they cared about was money, and they assumed everyone felt the same. Their kind always does."

"What's 'their kind'?" Ellery asked.

Nora didn't reply.

"Is Thomasina married?"

"No. Footloose and fancy free. That's our Thomasina."

It certainly seemed like their Thomasina, from the little Ellery had seen of her.

"Were she and Trevor ever..."

Nora looked approving. "Very good, dearie. We'll make a detective out of you yet."

Or a gossip columnist.

"Yes, they went out at one time. I think Trevor may have even proposed to her. I suppose they would have made a good team."

"Like Barnum and Bailey?" Ellery joked.

"I was thinking more of Bonnie and Clyde."

He must have looked taken aback because Nora said, "For a while there was quite a bit of speculation on whether they were running some kind of real-estate scam. Trevor would locate a property he was interested in purchasing, Tommy would contact the owners, negotiations would begin, and somehow the property always ended up being sold on terms advantageous to Trevor. Or, as in the case of the historical society, the property was condemned, and Trevor was able to buy the land for pennies."

"Did anyone ever look into these deals?"

"Not long after Chief Carson started nosing around, Trevor and Thomasina fell out."

"Romantically or professionally?"

"Both."

"Ah."

Nora tossed the brochure in the trash. She asked briskly, "Would you like me to dust the books in the glass cases?"

Another long day.

Though they weren't nearly as busy as on Monday, they did just about make enough to cover the lease. Nora was terrific with the customers who did wander in, which allowed Ellery to hide out in the back office, sorting books, instead of having to stay up front and onstage in the role of leading murder suspect.

At five fifteen, Nora called goodbye, told him not to stay too late, and departed, the jolly jingle of the front bell letting Ellery know he was finally alone in the shop.

"Try not to handle the letter any more than you already have. I'll be there in five."

Carson was there in four minutes.

He walked in, blew in, really, on a gust of salt-laced sea air. He spared one brief, assessing look for Ellery, who gave him a single thumb-up and then nodded at the letter lying facedown on the floor.

Carson slipped on blue Nitrile gloves, squatted down, and picked up the letter by the corner.

He read it, and his mouth thinned. He pulled out a plastic evidence bag, dropped the letter in, and rose.

"I'll have it dusted for prints and see if we can pull anything up. I can't offer you any guarantees, unfortunately."

Ellery folded his lips together. He nodded.

Carson hesitated. "I'm sorry. I'll have a word with Sue Lewis. I don't think she realizes what she's stirring up with those editorials."

Ellery nodded again.

"I don't think you're in any danger. This is someone... venting."

"Great."

Carson turned away, turned back. "It's...not a bad little town. In fact, overall, it's a nice place to live. Most of the time, people support each other and look out for each other."

"Sure," Ellery said tightly.

"But people are scared, and fear has a way of bringing out the worst in those who ought to know better. When this is all over—"

Ellery interrupted harshly, "When this is all over, I'll be back in New York and I'll never have to think about this place or these people ever again. It was a mistake to come here. A mistake to think I could ever fit—" He was able to cut off the rest of it, thankfully, but the words still echoed, naked in their hurt and fury.

After a moment, Carson nodded. "I'll let you know as soon as I find out anything."

He walked out, closing the door quietly behind him. Ellery watched his pale outline fade into the windy darkness.

He turned out the lamp, headed for the front door.

The bell rang sharply in the rough breeze as he pushed the door open. Ellery stepped out, locked the door, turned— and froze.

Someone stood motionless on the pavement, staring at him.

For a moment he couldn't seem to make sense of what he was seeing—of *who* he was seeing.

Trevor Maples.

CHAPTER FOURTEEN

"**Y**ou're Ellery Page?"

The voice was deeper, hair and eyebrows darker, but it could have been Trevor in the flesh.

"Yes." Ellery found his voice. "You're...Logan Maples."

"And you're the man suspected of murdering my brother."

There was a time that would have shocked him, hurt him. But now? He was like a punch-drunk boxer getting socked in the eye. He blinked, yes, but he barely felt it.

"I found him. That's all. There are several— I'm not the only— I had nothing to do with his death. I'm very sorry for your loss."

Maples ignored that. He was staring past Ellery at the darkened bookstore. "Is that where it happened?"

"Yes."

"May I see?"

Ellery hesitated. Logan Maples appeared to be as demanding and abrasive as his sibling, but after all, he had lost his brother to violence. If that didn't deserve some consideration, what did? He nodded, unlocked the door to the Crow's Nest, fumbled inside for the switch.

The hanging bell-shaped lights flared on, illuminating the tall shelves and sea paintings.

Maples brushed past him, striding toward the counter, walking right over the nearly invisible darkening in the floorboards.

Ellery said, "Er, I found him right there." He pointed to the center of the floor.

Maples turned and stared at the floorboards.

The truth was, there was really nothing to see, but Ellery kept a respectful silence. He couldn't help studying the other man. The resemblance was uncanny, though there were key differences. Trevor's hair had been a gingery red. Logan's was dark brown, with a few reddish glints. Trevor's eyes had been blue. Logan's were brown behind thick lenses.

"What exactly happened? The police department has been useless at giving information."

"That's because they don't know what exactly happened. They're still investigating."

"Ridiculous. He was slain with a sword from this store?"

"That seems to be the case. A sword used to hang over the doorway. It disappeared that night and hasn't been seen since."

Maples looked at the empty hooks above the doorway. "I can't understand it. Why would anyone do such a thing?"

Ellery wasn't sure if Maples was asking why would anyone kill Trevor—which by now felt like a rhetorical question—or if he was asking why Trevor had been killed in such a bizarre manner. The second question was the one that haunted Ellery. He kept a diplomatic silence.

Finally, Maples surreptitiously rubbed his knuckles against his nose and faced Ellery. "Thank you for allowing me this moment."

"Of course," Ellery replied. "I'm afraid I didn't know your brother well. I didn't even realize he had a brother. Let alone a twin."

"We aren't—weren't—twins. I'm two years older than Trevor." Logan's dark eyes fastened on Ellery's. "It's only fair to tell you that if you did have anything to do with my brother's death, I'll make it my mission to see you spend the rest of your life in prison."

"I don't have any brothers or sisters, but I'm sure I'd feel the same way," Ellery said.

They walked toward the entrance. Ellery held the door for Maples. "Is there anything else I can do?"

"No." Maples stepped outside and turned to give him an icy smile. "If local gossip is to be believed, you've done enough already."

He did the drive home on autopilot.

By nature, Ellery was optimistic and confident, but he'd be lying if he tried to pretend that the last few days hadn't knocked the stuffing out of him. Every day seemed to bring some new and worse disaster—as if being suspected of killing someone wasn't bad enough. Where would it stop? With him bankrupt? With him incarcerated? With him dead too?

At this point, nothing seemed impossible. Or at least, nothing bad seemed impossible. The good things were what seemed to be in scarce supply in his life.

Maybe he *should* cut his losses and go back to New York?

Sell the bookshop to Janet, auction off the contents of Captain's Seat—the Museum of Ugly Art would probably jump at the chance to add some of those pieces to its collection—let Tommy Rider turn Captain's Seat into condominiums.

A guy could only take so much, and Ellery was reaching his breaking point.

Nobody in Pirate's Cove would shed a tear if he left, that was for sure.

And yet it went against the grain to simply give up.

He had never met his great-great-great-aunt Eudora. Frankly, she sounded like a little bit of a nut, but she had wanted him—the last surviving Page—to carry on whatever was left of their family heritage. Until he had inherited Captain's Seat and the bookshop, he'd had no idea he even had a family heritage. Heck, he hadn't known he had a great-great-great-aunt Eudora.

Well, the family heritage was Great-great-great-aunt Eudora's thing, not his. He wasn't obliged to take on the burden of a past he'd probably disapprove of anyway. And yet, the fact that it had meant so much to her, that she'd considered pulling up stakes a couple of times but had always resisted, had hung on until the very end—and then passed that faint, flickering torch to him—it meant something.

Or maybe he just wanted, *needed*, it to mean something.

The truth was, he'd been directionless for the past few years. Oh, he'd worked hard at different things and he'd saved up, but he had never been sure what he was working toward or what he was saving for. And then things with Todd had fallen apart, and he'd felt...adrift. Like what was the point of any of it? Not in a dramatic long-walk-off-a-short-pier kind of way, but more like cue Peggy Whatsherface *Is That All There Is?*

And then Mr. Landry had phoned to tell him about Pirate's Cove and Captain's Seat and the Crow's Nest, and it had seemed like a nudge from the cosmos. Like maybe this was what he'd been waiting for without even realizing it.

But if *this* was what he'd been waiting for, he must have done something very bad in a previous life.

He had planned on painting the dining room that evening, but by the time he reached home—okay, not home, Captain's Seat—he found he had no enthusiasm for renovations.

Instead, he poured himself a glass of wine and sat down at the dining-room table to play his version of Solitaire Scrabble.

He had the SCRABBLE Slam! card game, and different phone apps, of course, as well as a couple of electronic programs for his laptop, but his favorite method was to use a regular board, tiles, and a timer, and simply play against himself. He found it soothing.

Not just soothing. A way to analyze and work through his problems without consciously trying to do that very thing. The words that popped up during this particular mental exercise were always interesting. Sometimes even uncanny. So he was hoping for similar results that evening.

After everything he'd been through over the past few days, he wouldn't have been surprised with Ouija-board-like results, and at first it did seem like his unconscious was pulling at the threads of his anxieties. He got PIRATES (nine points) and then NUANCES (nine points) right off the bat, with an additional one hundred points for twice in a row using all his tiles. Then a lot of, well, scrabbling before he finally he got QUIXOTIC (seventy-six points!).

He began to feel calmer. The wine probably helped. He could not claim that his thinking was much clearer, but he did manage to get a little perspective.

Yes, some people thought he was capable of murder, but Jack Carson didn't seem to be one of them. Not that Jack—Chief Carson—had come right out and said so, but he had said he didn't think Ellery had committed *this* murder. Small victories.

That was very sad about his wife. About the childhood-sweethearts thing. It was very confusing too, because Ellery would have almost bet money that Chief Carson's default was not heterosexual. Granted, sexuality was complex. One size did *not* fit all.

He was getting up to pour himself a third glass, when he stepped on the hard plastic wiffle ball he had used to play with the puppy that morning, and nearly fell.

He managed to save himself by grabbing the sideboard. The mahogany cabinet was too big to move, but he jarred the pewter candelabra at the far end. The candelabra rocked and then fell with a huge crash. Ellery went to retrieve it. He was thinking how heavy it was—and that it would make a good murder weapon—when he noticed there was something odd about the wall. He set the candelabra down and peered more closely.

He wasn't imagining it: there seemed to be a narrow gap in the dark paneling.

Rain damage? Rotting wood? But no. As he looked more closely, he realized it was an opening.

An opening indicating a doorway?

An opening indicating a space behind the wall?

"A secret passage?" He laughed in disbelief.

But really, if ever a house was perfect for a secret passage, it would be Captain's Seat.

He felt around for a latch or a button, but there was nothing. Then it occurred to him to press against the panel itself, and sure enough, the board sprang forward, revealing a doorway—and a secret passage beyond.

Or at least, he was hoping for a secret passage. It was too dark to be sure what he was looking at. He thought he caught the very faint whiff of plastic and mothballs.

He hurried into the kitchen, retrieved one of the flashlights he'd replaced batteries in after his trip to the hardware store, and returned to the dining room. He shone the flashlight into the doorway and saw that it was not a secret passage after all.

Nor even a secret room.

It was a closet.

A neatly concealed but perfectly ordinary coat closet.

Wha-wha-wha. Cue the Fail Trumpet.

A tweed walking hat sat on a very dusty shelf. A couple of outdated raincoats hung limply from a wooden bar. A pair of galoshes faced the back corner as though in trouble for splashing through the mud still caked on their soles.

In the very back were two cardboard boxes that turned out to be stuffed with old magazines.

Those would probably be entertaining to look through. Depending on what condition they were in, he might even consider selling them at the Crow's Nest. But sorting through the delights of moldering, mildewed magazines would have to wait for another night. Ellery was finally tired enough to try sleeping.

As he shoved the boxes of magazines against the wall of the dining room, he heard a scraping sound inside the closet, and then a metal chime as something banged down on the wooden floor.

Something had been wedged behind the boxes, and with their removal, had fallen free. He turned the flashlight back on, directing its beam into the black interior.

He thought for a moment he was looking at some kind of cane or walking stick. Then he saw the etching and realized he was looking at a blade. A blade he had seen before. A blade now stained with a reddish-brown substance that raised the hair on his head.

He sank down to the floor, telling himself he needed to get a better look, but in fact, his knees had given out. He crawled forward, and the beam of the flashlight wavered like moth wings because his hand was shaking.

A sword. A cutlass. The very one that had once hung above the door at the Crow's Nest. The very one used to murder Trevor Maples.

CHAPTER FIFTEEN

Ellery's breath caught in his throat. He backed out of the closet as hastily as if he'd discovered a body.

In a way, he had.

How the… This was *impossible*. How did it get there? Wrong question. Who could have put it there? Someone with access to Captain's Seat. Someone who knew about the hidden closet. Someone who definitely had it in for him, definitely wanted to see him take the blame for Trevor's murder.

His mind was spinning—with about the same results as tires stuck in mud.

This looked bad. This *was* bad. *So* bad. The murder weapon discovered in his home, in his closet—his *hidden* closet? His heart pounded with sick certainty. He could visualize the story in the *Scuttlebutt Weekly*. He would be arrested. *Of course* he would be arrested. He would arrest himself at this point!

What should he do? What *could* he do?

Strangely enough, the first idea that came to him was to phone Chief Carson.

He rejected that thought almost instantly.

Even if Carson believed him, believed that someone was trying to frame him, he wouldn't have any choice but to arrest Ellery. He had already admitted he had to follow the evidence wherever it led.

No, Ellery would have to get rid of the sword. Hide it somewhere it would never be found. Or at least hide it somewhere where it couldn't incriminate him.

Where?

Think.

He could throw it into the ocean. He could bury it in the woods. He could bury it in a meadow. He could hide it in one of the falling-down barns or cowsheds outside the village. He could take it back to the Crow's Nest. The police would never search the shop a second time. What did it matter *where*, so long as he got it off his property?

His panicked thoughts raced from possibility to possibility.

And then, thankfully, reason asserted itself.

Someone had deliberately planted this sword in his house to implicate him in Trevor's murder. It was unlikely that, having taken that risk, this unknown person's plan stopped there. They couldn't know when or even if Ellery would stumble upon the sword, so there had to be another phase to this plan. Like an anonymous phone call to the police?

Counterintuitive though it might feel, his best defense was to contact the police first, himself. That was what an innocent person would do, and he was an innocent person. Therefore, as much as he dreaded the idea, he needed to call Chief Carson and report this—and the sooner, the better. If he didn't, it would only make him look guiltier.

Thank God his sense of self-preservation had kicked in to stop him from touching or moving the sword.

Ellery rifled through the contents of his wallet, found Carson's card, and phoned his direct line at the police department.

This time there was no reply, so it appeared even Carson had to occasionally go home to sleep.

Ellery tried the next number on the card. The phone on the other end rang twice, and then someone picked up.

"Carson." The voice was thick and gravelly.

Ellery glanced at the clock and was startled to realize it was after one in the morning.

"Chief, I'm sorry to wake you, but something just happened." He added, "Sorry. I should have said. It's me, Ellery Page."

"I know it's you, Ellery." Carson sounded like someone trying to hold on to their patience. "What's happened now?"

"I just found the murder weapon."

"You…" He could practically see Carson blinking, but to alertness. "Did you say—"

"There's a hidden closet in the dining room. The sword was in there."

He heard what sounded like the rustle of bedclothes. Carson said in a completely wide-awake voice, "I'm on my way. Don't touch anything."

He hung up.

Ellery must have covered several miles, pacing up and down the long entry hall, before the front door suddenly jumped beneath a hard fist.

Carson's voice sounded muted behind the thick planks. "Ellery? It's Chief Carson."

Ellery leaped to open the door.

He was expecting several police cars and the state CSI team, so it was a surprise to see only Carson, hair ruffled, chin stubbled, wearing jeans and a heavy sheepskin coat. Ellery peered past him.

"You came alone?"

"Yes." Carson's face was grim. "Show me where you found the sword."

Ellery led the way to the dining room and stood aside as Carson pulled on his gloves and leaned into the closet to have a look.

"It looks like blood on the blade." Ellery felt sick, remembering.

Carson was silent for what seemed like a long time.

When he ducked out again, his expression was not encouraging.

Ellery rushed in before Carson could speak. "I know how this looks, but I swear to you, I didn't even know this closet existed until about an hour ago. Someone is trying to frame me."

It sounded ridiculous, but what other explanation could there be? Not that he expected Carson to believe him.

"Even if I had killed Trevor—and why would I? I had nothing to gain from his death, *no* motive—why would I go out of my way to do all these things that make me look guilty? Why would I kill him in my own shop? Why would I use my own sword? Why would I hide the sword where it would further incriminate me? None of this makes sense, and I understand you have to follow the evidence, but I also know *you* don't think any of this makes sense either. You *can't*."

"I agree."

Ellery, getting his breath and preparing to follow up his line of argument, fell silent. He said slowly, "You...agree?"

Carson said crisply, "Yes. I agree. None of this makes sense. You're being set up."

"You see it too?" Ellery felt almost weak with relief. "You believe me?"

Carson's mouth curved sardonically. "Did you think I wouldn't?"

"Well, frankly, yes. The evidence against me keeps mounting."

"Conveniently, that evidence is solely circumstantial. You're perfectly right about your lack of motive. Not that motive is always crucial, but in this case—and given your background—we need something more to explain why you'd suddenly decide to kill Maples. Especially in such an impractical and overly complicated way."

"Given my background?" Ellery echoed.

"Correct. I did tell you we'd be investigating you."

Yes, Carson had said something about a background check. Ellery had been thinking work history and credit report, but maybe it had been more extensive.

Carson was saying, "There's nothing in your history that indicates any tendency toward violent or criminal behavior. Even your ex-boyfriend says you're a nice enough guy."

Nice enough guy? High praise indeed!

Ellery sputtered, "You sp-p-poke to Todd?"

Carson shrugged. "That's how it works. We spoke to your employers, your friends, your neighbors, your agent, and your ex. You don't have a criminal record—unless we want to count an ungodly number of parking tickets—and we checked your credit and employment history, your—"

"You talked to my *agent*?"

"That actually worked to your benefit because according to Ms. Samuelson, you're a phenomenally terrible actor."

Ellery's jaw dropped.

"I'll be honest," Carson said. "The fact that you were an actor did initially bias me, but I've seen for myself that you're a very bad liar."

"Well!" Ellery huffed. He was offended but, of course, also relieved.

"In short, despite the wealth of circumstantial evidence, I can't come up with a believable theory as to why you'd suddenly murder a man you barely knew. Even early on, the very fact that there was so much circumstantial evidence seemed suspicious. Homicide investigations aren't usually solved so easily. Finding the sword here, thrown in the back of a closet, is the final straw."

"Why is someone doing this to me?" Ellery whispered.

Carson didn't answer for a second or two. Then he said, "I'd like to be able to reassure you that you just happen to be a convenient scapegoat, but it does seem more personal than that."

"It feels more personal."

"Can you think of anyone in Pirate's Cove who might have a grudge against you?"

"No. I'd never met any of these people—never knew they even existed—until I moved here."

"Anyone you've had a run-in with? Has anyone exhibited hostile or aggressive behavior toward you?"

"You mean besides Sue Lewis?"

Carson looked pained. "I think Sue's real grudge is against the police department."

Ellery remembered Nora's shared insight into Sue's motivations and held his tongue.

"Trevor and I argued about the bookshop, but that wasn't personal."

"It wouldn't seem so on the surface," agreed Carson.

"Could this have something to do with the Crow's Nest? Trevor wanted to buy me out. Now Janet Maples has offered to buy the bookshop." He half joked, "Maybe the store's sitting on buried treasure."

"You're not completely wrong. You're sitting on some of the most valuable real estate in Pirate's Cove. The Crow's

He watched from the doorway as Carson got into his vehicle, turned on the engine. The headlights flashed on, illuminating the beds of dead flowers in the front garden. Carson reversed in a driving-manual-perfect arc and drove away down the road.

Ellery watched until the red taillights disappeared. He closed the door, locked it, double-checked the locks, and went upstairs to bed.

Brushing his teeth in the drafty master bedroom, he considered the very large bed, its size serving to stress how empty it was. Legend had it, Captain Horatio Page had died—at the ripe old age of 102—alone in that bed.

Hopefully the mattress had been changed once or twice in the interim.

Tomorrow he would go to Vincent Veterinary Hospital and see about retrieving his little orphan buddy. It would be nice to have some company in this house.

In the meantime…

Ellery finished brushing his teeth, turned off the lights, and climbed into the boat-sized bed.

CHAPTER SIXTEEN

He did not sleep well.

Every time a beam creaked, a tree branch scratched against the window, or the wind whispered down the chimney, Ellery's eyes popped open, and he'd spend the next four or five minutes listening for stealthy, approaching footsteps.

The footsteps did not come, but memories did.

On the whole, murderous intruders might have been preferable.

Twenty minutes after Ellery *finally* fell asleep, his alarm clock went off.

Nor did the day improve once he reached the village.

The receptionist at Vincent Veterinary Hospital delivered the bad news that the puppy had been adopted.

"Already?" Ellery protested.

She looked apologetic. "The Harmons lost their family dog yesterday, and the kids were desperate for a new puppy. The little guy will be well cared for, well loved, don't you worry."

"Sure," Ellery said. "That's great news."

And really, it *was* great news. The puppy had gone to a good home, where he'd get lots of attention and wasn't liable to be a civilian casualty of the war on Ellery. True, Ellery felt a little heartbroken, but he wasn't ten years old, was he? The world was full of puppies needing a good home if he *really* wanted a dog.

When Nora arrived at the Crow's Nest, she was almost bubbling with news.

"You've been replaced on the front page of the *Scuttlebutt*, dearie," she informed Ellery.

"Is that true?" He felt a wave of relief. "Why? What's happened?"

"Cyrus Jones has moved up in the polls. He's now leading the race for mayor."

"*Oh.* Okay." Ellery didn't really have strong feelings either way about who should be mayor, but the citizens of Pirate's Cove did seem to take the race seriously.

Nora wasn't done. "*And* Trevor Maples left everything to his twin brother!"

Ellery opened his mouth, remembered he wasn't supposed to know anything about Trevor's will, and said instead, "Was that unexpected?"

"As a time bomb," Nora gloated. "Janet Maples expected everything to go to her. She's insisting the will has to be a forgery. The paper ran a special-edition interview with her."

Janet must have believed she had removed the only copy of the will when she broke into Trevor's house. It seemed that Chief Carson had not challenged her regarding the missing document. What a shock when Trevor's brother showed up with his own copy. Maybe that was what the chief had been waiting for: Janet's reaction.

One thing could not be overlooked. Janet's belief that she was going to inherit all of Trevor's worldly possessions gave her a strong motive for murder.

"Why would she think Trevor was leaving everything to her? Didn't they have a really contentious divorce?"

"Yep." Nora looked thoughtful. "I'm wondering if they had some arrangement, though. It's no secret Trevor always wanted to get his hands on Old Salt Stationery. Maybe Janet agreed to leave everything to Trevor if Trevor agreed to leave everything to her. It would be just like Trevor to double-cross her."

"I heard from someone that the only person Trevor ever cared about was his brother."

Actually, he'd heard that from Janet.

Nora said, "I don't know. I never met the brother."

"I met him last night. Didn't they grow up in Pirate's Cove?"

Nora stared at Ellery in astonishment. "You met him last night?"

Ellery nodded. "He came by as I was closing up. He wanted to see where...it happened."

Nora shivered. "That's a little morbid, if you ask me."

Ellery shrugged. People grieved in different ways, but everybody needed closure.

"But no," Nora said suddenly. "The Maples didn't grow up here. Trevor moved to Pirate's Cove when he married Janet. Janet grew up here."

"I see."

"Of course, you'd *think* Trevor had grown up here, the way he acted. Like he owned the whole village. I guess he was trying his best to do that very thing. I wonder if the brother will sell off all his holdings. Did he give you any idea last night?"

"No. I only spoke to him for a couple of minutes. He did mention they're not twins. He's a few years older than Trevor."

Nora looked thoughtful. "When you think about it, *there's* someone with a motive for murder. Twin or not twin. Trevor was a rich man."

Ellery smiled, but yes, he had been thinking the same thing.

Whether it was because Pirate's Cove had a new favorite main suspect in the Maples murder or some other reason, business picked up again that morning. It was a promising sign, but Ellery couldn't help fearing that it was too little, too late.

"We have to find a way to lure more people into the store," Nora said when they finally broke for a late lunch. Ellery had bought sandwiches, tea, and cupcakes from the little café down the street to celebrate Nora's employment, and Nora had gotten teary-eyed over this small attention.

"That sounds a little sinister," Ellery teased.

"I'm serious. I was thinking about this last night. We should start a mystery group."

"What kind of mystery group?" With everything going on, maybe it wasn't surprising his first thought was Nora meant some kind of amateur sleuthing club (he'd spent a lot of time reshelving titles in the cozy-mystery section that morning).

"We could try a two-pronged approach," Nora mused. "Start one group for writers and one group for readers. If we could turn the Crow's Nest into a social center, we'd get more traffic, and if we get more traffic, we'll get more business. It's simply the law of averages."

"I'm all for that," Ellery said. "But how would it work? Do you think there are that many mystery readers in Pirate's Cove?"

"Not yet. There will be."

"Why will there be?"

Nora's eyes sparkled. "Haven't you noticed how little there is to do in the village? There's the Salty Dog and the theater. That's about it. Oh, and the Women's Club. People here are dying for entertainment. If we start a reading group, we'll get members. I guarantee it."

Ellery studied her. Her cheeks were pink, her eyes bright. Her enthusiasm was contagious.

"Not only that, we've got more room than the Toy Chest. Maybe we could do something in conjunction with Mr. Carter. Maybe the Monday Night Scrabblers could meet here instead of next door."

"I guess I could ask."

"Yes! What do we have to lose?" Nora said.

Once again, Ellery reflected that hiring Nora was probably the best move he could have made for the health and welfare of the Crow's Nest. He said slowly, "I like that idea, but all my free time is taken up with remodeling Captain's Seat. Would you be up for running these new groups?"

Nora looked astonished and then delighted. "*Yes!*"

"All right, then. You've convinced me. Let's give it a try." Ellery hid his smile in his cup of tea.

Late afternoon, they received a surprise visit.

Ellery was in his office, browsing the Advanced Book Exchange website to try to figure out how to price some of the vintage paperbacks Great-great-great-aunt Eudora had been stockpiling in the cellar, when Nora poked her head in his office.

"He's here!" she hissed.

"Who's here?"

"Him. Logan Maples. He wants to talk to you."

Ellery stopped smiling. His good mood deflated. This could not be good.

"Show him back here," he said. If Logan was going to start shouting at him, it would be better behind closed doors.

A moment later Nora ushered Logan into Ellery's office.

Now that Ellery could see Logan in the light of day, the resemblance between him and Trevor really was remarkable, but they weren't identical. Nor were the differences all physical. Logan did not share his brother's taste for ostentatious jewelry or flashy clothes. His hair was cut in a short, no-nonsense style. He wore thick horn-rim glasses. He looked older and more severe than Trevor; however, his smile was wide and seemed surprisingly genuine.

Trevor had always smiled like he knew something you didn't.

"Thank you for seeing me," Logan said.

"Of course," Ellery replied, as if he had never considered trying to wriggle out through the tiny bathroom window.

"I feel like I may owe you an apology. I've been speaking to Police Chief Carson. He told me that the editor of the local paper has a vendetta against the police department, and you've been caught in the crossfire. He said you're no longer considered a suspect in my brother's death."

This was news to Ellery. "He said that?"

"You seem surprised."

"I'm not surprised I'm no longer a suspect. I'm surprised the chief came right out and admitted it." That wasn't completely true, of course. Even after the previous evening, Ellery *was* surprised that Carson considered him completely cleared of suspicion. Carson did not seem like the trusting type.

"I got the impression he's very unhappy with the local paper."

"He's not the only one."

Logan said, "I can't entirely fault the paper. It's upsetting the police haven't made an arrest yet. But I've no wish to see the wrong person punished. And it seems you've come in for an unfair share of abuse."

What would be a fair share of abuse? But, obviously, Ellery didn't say that.

"Thank you. I appreciate your saying so. I know this has to be awful for you."

"You can't imagine."

"Were you and Trevor close?" Ellery asked.

"Yes. We didn't see each other as much as we would have liked, especially in recent years. He was always trying to convince me to buy a vacation home on the island. I travel a lot for my work, so it didn't seem practical."

"What is it you do?" Ellery asked.

"I'm Director of Sales for Aegis Futures. We're a national leader in assisted living and memory care with high-performing communities all across the United States."

"Wow," Ellery said, having only the vaguest idea of what that meant.

"Ironically, I had just made the decision to take early retirement before this happened. Trevor was scouting potential vacation properties for me."

"I'm so sorry."

"The best-laid plans, as they say." For a moment Logan stared into some bleak and unknown vista.

"Then you *are* moving to Pirate's Cove?" Ellery asked, watching him.

"I can't imagine living here year-round, no, but it's a lovely vacation spot, and the town is a very good financial investment."

That sounded all-encompassing. Ellery said tentatively, "The town is?"

"Yes. Trevor was a genius when it came to investing in real estate. He owns—owned—half of Pirate's Cove at the time of his death."

"I had no idea."

"Didn't you?" Logan raised his brows. "Oh, but then you're new to the area yourself, I understand."

"Yes. My great-great-great-aunt died and left me her house and this bookshop."

"So I heard. In fact, I wanted to speak to you about the bookshop. Apparently, you and Trevor were in negotiations for the property at the time of his death. I want you to know that I will still honor the terms of that deal."

"That's kind," Ellery said. "But there was no deal. I don't want to sell."

Logan stared. "You don't?"

"No."

"But I was given to understand you do plan to sell."

"I don't. I have no intention of selling. I told Trevor that the afternoon he died."

"Even after everything that's happened?"

"Even now."

Logan said slowly, "Forgive me for asking, but does this have something to do with Janet?"

"Trevor's ex-wife? No."

Logan looked unconvinced. "Did Janet offer to buy this property?"

"Yes, but I turned her down. I don't want to sell."

"I'm sure," Logan said in the tone of one who is far from sure. "If I may be blunt, any offer Janet made was likely based on the false assumption she would inherit Trevor's estate. Why she would imagine such a thing, I've no idea. It's hard to envision a more corrosive divorce than theirs. But in the brief time I've been in Pirate's Cove, it's become clear to me that Janet not only had designs on Trevor's property, she may have even been involved in his death."

Having been on the receiving end of rumor, speculation, and a downright smear campaign, Ellery was hesitant to respond, even though he had his own serious doubts about Janet Maples.

"You didn't get that from Chief Carson," he said.

"No. Chief Carson displayed an alarming unwillingness—or perhaps inability—to discuss possible suspects."

"Anything else would be irresponsible." Ellery was surprised at how much he resented criticism of Chief Carson.

Logan said quietly, "That's easy to say when you're not the one who lost your only remaining family."

"I'm sorry," Ellery said. "I know this must be terrible."

"Yes. It is."

"Then you're not planning to sell Trevor's property holdings?"

"Certainly not. Trevor wouldn't have wanted that."

That was probably true. Trevor had been nothing if not acquisitive.

Logan rose. "It seems I've been misinformed. If you do change your mind about selling, please let me know. I assure you no one can give you a better price than I."

Ellery also rose, offering his hand. "Thank you. I'll keep that in mind."

They shook. Trevor had been one of those guys who shook hands like it was the preliminary to arm wrestling. Logan did the two-finger thing, as though he feared catching something contagious.

"Good. I hope you won't be offended if I say that it would be wise to also keep in mind that Janet is dangerous."

"Dangerous?" Ellery repeated. He wasn't arguing; he was considering.

"Yes. Trevor was too much the gentlemen to reveal secrets, but it wasn't hard to read between the lines. I've heard her story now is that she and Trevor were planning to get back together. I know for a fact that's a lie. She can't be trusted. If you're smart, you'll steer clear of her."

"I appreciate the advice," Ellery said politely. He had been trying not to judge Logan based on his dislike of Trevor, and he believed he had succeeded. He disliked Logan for his own obnoxious self.

CHAPTER SEVENTEEN

"**S**hoo," Nora said.

"You're sure you don't mind closing up?"

"SHOOO!" she repeated more loudly, and Ellery shooed.

He had been waiting all afternoon for a chance to slip away and talk to Chief Carson, but business had stayed steady, and he hadn't felt right leaving Nora—even though Nora was probably more capable of running the shop without him than he'd be without her.

He was on his way out the door when he nearly crashed into Tommy Rider.

He apologized, reaching out to steady her.

"Where's the fire?" Tommy laughed. And then, "Hey, are you free for drinks? I was thinking we could go over to the Salty Dog."

Ellery hesitated. "I'd love that, but I have to talk to Chief Carson."

Her brows rose. "Anything urgent?"

"Uh, no. Nothing urgent."

"Then phone him from the pub."

Yeee-ah. *No.* No way was he talking to Carson with every ear in the Salty Dog turned his way like a field of satellite dishes primed to overhear interstellar communications.

"Maybe I can meet you later?" he suggested.

She hesitated. "Sure. Let's say six?"

"Okay."

He was starting to move past her, but Tommy said casually, "Who was that in your shop earlier?"

He was happy to be able to answer, "When? There were a lot of people in the shop today."

"Right. I mean, was that Trevor's brother I saw leaving here about three thirty?"

"Yeah. That was Logan Maples."

"I thought it must be. They could be twins. The resemblance is…uncanny." She seemed genuinely shaken.

"Yeah, it's a little startling. You never met him?"

"No."

"Personality-wise, they're not that much alike."

"I believe it. Trevor used to say Logan was all work and no play."

Ellery remembered that, according to Nora, once upon a time Trevor and Tommy had been an item. Tommy was probably a wellspring of information on the topic of Trevor. He said, "Trevor was no slouch in that department either, I gather. Logan said he owned half of the village at the time of his death."

Tommy's smile faded a little. Her eyes avoided his. "Yes. Close. Trevor was shrewd when it came to investing in real estate."

"Some of the credit has to go to you, doesn't it?"

Her expression changed, grew almost wary. "What's that supposed to mean?"

"Isn't that how you two got together? I just assumed you worked as a team. You're the best real-estate agent in Pirate's Cove."

"Someone's been listening to gossip," Tommy said tartly.

Ellery smiled. "Well, yeah, Nora Sweeny works in my shop. I'm up on *all* the local gossip now."

After a moment, Tommy's scowl faded. She snorted. "I believe it. The old busybody. I suppose she's still bitter about the Carmichael School."

At Ellery's blank look, Tommy said, "Please. She must have told you how Trevor and I connived and schemed to get the old schoolhouse condemned so that the historical society was forced out into the sunlight where all the vampires burned up and blew away." She added darkly, "All but one."

Whoa. Someone else sounded a little bitter herself.

"Nora did say something about the historical society folding when they lost their venue."

"I'll bet." Tommy glanced past him to where Nora was rearranging the book display in the front window.

Nora met their gazes, sniffed in disapproval—they didn't need to hear her to interpret that expression—and turned her attention back to the books.

"So childish." Tommy's tone was withering. "Anyway, we didn't do anything illegal. The building should have been condemned long before that. And it wasn't personal, for heaven's sake. It was just business."

"Small towns, small minds," Ellery said, like he was an expert on village life.

"Exactly! I suppose the old bat also told you I broke up Trevor's marriage? Well, *that* is a lie. He and Janet were through long before I came along."

Yeah, sure. That was probably what Jerry said about Todd and Ellery. But water under the bridge. This wasn't about Ellery; it was about finding something to help narrow down the field of suspects in Trevor's murder. Because even if he wasn't Chief Carson's prime suspect, he was still under suspicion as far as most of the village was concerned. For sure as far as Sue Lewis's subscribers were concerned.

"Do you think Janet could have had anything to do with Trevor's death?" he asked.

Tommy brightened, started to answer, and then stopped. She made a face. "*Could* she kill Trevor? Sure. There've been times *I* wanted to kill Trevor. *Did* she? I find it very hard to believe she'd have done it like that. For one thing, why drag you into it? For another, how would she even—"

She broke off with a strange expression.

"How would she even what?" Ellery asked.

Tommy glanced at him, but he thought she didn't actually see him.

"You mean the sword?" he pressed. "How would she know it was in the shop? How would she get it down? How would he not see that coming?"

Tommy was still looking at him like he was speaking in a foreign language. She said abruptly, "I'm sorry, Ellery. I just remembered I'm supposed to be meeting a client. We'll talk later. See you at the pub."

She turned and strode down the street toward her office.

* * * * *

"You think Logan Maples murdered his brother for his money?" Chief Carson inquired in the tone of one striving to be polite in trying circumstances.

"I didn't say *that*," Ellery said hastily.

He had been sitting in Chief Carson's office, waiting for the chief to finish dealing with the mayor, the state police, off-island news agencies, and Sue Lewis.

After the phone call with Lewis, Carson's mood had definitely taken a turn for the worse, though he had remained courteous—if terse—throughout the conversation. He was still courteous, but it was obvious he felt he didn't have time to spend chatting with Ellery.

"You were asking about Maples's will," Carson said. "Presumably that's what you're getting at."

"Okay, yes. Maybe Trevor's murder was just a simple case of greed, and the sword and the pirate costume and the fact that the murder took place in my shop are just...distractions. Stage props."

Carson said crisply, "First, the murder didn't take place in your shop."

"It...didn't?"

"No. The crime scene was staged in your shop, but technically Maples was killed at another, still unknown, location. Second, he was drugged before he was stabbed."

"Drugged?" Ellery echoed. "I don't understand."

"Third—"

"Wait. Was the pirate sword even the murder weapon?" Ellery asked.

"Yes and no. The sword went through Maples's heart, killing him instantly, but he was already dying. He had ingested a fatal dose of benzodiazepines and alcohol."

"Why was there so much blood, then? If he was nearly dead by the time he was run through—"

"Blood thinners."

"He was on blood thinners?"

"Apparently so."

Ellery's lips parted. He had no idea what to say. He wasn't even sure what all this meant, besides the fact that it proved Trevor's death had definitely been premeditated.

Carson said with grim finality, "And *third*, Maples was broke."

"*Broke?*"

"You heard me."

"But I thought he owned half of Pirate's Cove."

"More like a third. But it's called being land-poor. Most of the businesses Trevor owned were not turning a profit. And those that were profitable, were not profitable year-round."

"What about the antiques store? What about Gimcrack Antiques?"

Carson's smile was sardonic. "There are two things Pirate's Cove has an endless supply of: salt water and antiques. The whole damned town is an antique. Gimcrack Antiques relied on the tourist trade as much or more than his other businesses."

Now that was a shocker. Trevor had always behaved like he had money to burn.

"What about his house?" Ellery asked.

"The most valuable asset he had was that house, but it too is mortgaged to the hilt."

"Wow. I had no idea."

"No one did. Including his ex-wife." Carson sighed. "And on the topic of Janet Maples, I spoke to Jonas Landry, Maples's lawyer, and it's true that until recently, Maples's will did still leave everything to Mrs. Maples, but then a month ago he altered the will to the benefit of his brother, Logan."

"That can't be a coincidence."

"Actually, it can. Before his marriage, Maples's will left everything to the brother. It makes sense that after his divorce he'd change his will back."

"But the timing. Why then? Now. You don't think it's suspicious that he waited five years, but then a month before he's murdered, he changes his will back?"

"It raises several flags, yes, but it doesn't prove anything. When you've been in law enforcement as long as I have, you learn that coincidences happen."

Ellery was silent, thinking this over. An officer came in and spoke to Carson, throwing Ellery a curious look. Carson signed some papers, nodded at the officer, who departed, and then the chief turned his attention back to Ellery.

"Anything else?"

"Yes. Just because Trevor turned out to be broke doesn't mean he wasn't killed for his wealth. If everyone *thought* he was rich, then gain is still a motive."

"You're absolutely correct," Carson said—he even sounded approving. "But in this case, it seems that Logan Maples did know his brother's financial situation. He brought it up the first time I interviewed him. Also, Trevor's phone records indicate he spoke to his brother regularly, which further confirms Logan's story that they were in close contact."

"Well, that's disappointing," Ellery admitted.

Carson laughed. "I take it you don't like the brother?"

"No. I don't. I wasn't crazy about Trevor, and I like Logan even less. He seems...I don't know. Cold-blooded."

"He might be, but that's not a crime."

Another officer came in with a small white pizza box. "Here's your dinner, Chief."

"Thanks."

The officer withdrew, closing the door behind him.

Carson opened the box, and the mouthwatering fragrance of Italian cheese, tomato sauce, and sausage filled the room.

Ellery's stomach growled. Loudly.

Carson raised his eyebrows. "Pardon? Did you say something?"

Ellery laughed, shook his head, and rose. "No. I'll leave you to have your dinner in peace."

"That would be a novelty." Carson was smiling too. His eyes looked almost turquoise in the office light. "Come on.

Pull up a chair. Might as well have a slice. You can share the rest of your crime theories, Mr. Brown."

Ellery hesitated. He really shouldn't stay. He was supposed to meet Tommy at the Salty Dog in ten minutes. Then again, he could always text her and say he was running a little late. It wasn't like Tommy didn't know anyone in the pub. The miracle would be if she didn't know *everyone*. He sat down again and scooted his chair closer to the desk. "Mr. Brown?"

"Encyclopedia Brown. I thought you owned a mystery bookstore?"

"That's a fluke."

"Ah. Okay. But didn't you read those books when you were a kid?"

"I'm not sure. Was he the one with the girl friend bodyguard who could beat everyone up?"

"That's right. Sally Kimball."

Ellery's grin was crooked as he reached for a slice of pizza. "Now I remember. Even back then I wanted Sally to be a boy."

Carson's eyes met his. He lifted a slice, caught a dangling string of cheese with his tongue, said, "There's nothing wrong with girls." He took a full bite of pizza and added thickly, "Nothing wrong with boys either."

Ellery nearly swallowed pizza backward. Was Carson—? Was that a loaded comment? Carson's gaze still held his, but his expression was bland, unreadable.

"I like girls," Ellery agreed. "Some of my best friends are girls."

Carson started to reply, but someone banged on the door to his office.

"*Chief! Chief?*"

Carson straightened in his chair. "Come in," he yelled, maybe more forcefully than necessary.

The door flew open, and Officer Martin leaned in and said, "Chief! Thomasina Rider was just found dead in her office. It looks like she's been murdered!"

CHAPTER EIGHTEEN

What a day.

What a night.

What the hell?

Once upon a time he had been an ordinary guy living an ordinary life.

Now?

Now he was giving Jessica Fletcher—as well as Encyclopedia Brown—a run for their money.

And people in Pirate's Cove had the gall to talk about the crime in New York City!

Ellery mentally shook his head as he climbed the stairs to the front door of Captain's Seat. After the terrible news had come through about Tommy Rider, Jack Carson hadn't been able to get Ellery out of his office fast enough. Ellery had barely had a chance to tell Jack—Chief Carson—about the odd way Tommy had acted when they had been discussing Janet's possible involvement in Trevor's murder.

That wasn't the troubling part. The troubling part was that, even after learning someone he knew—someone he was supposed to have drinks with that evening—had been found murdered, he'd spent most of the drive home wondering if Jack Carson had been trying to tell him something.

Something beyond how much he'd loved the Encyclopedia Brown books as a kid.

Was it possible Jack Carson was bisexual?

It kind of made sense because when Ellery had first met Chief Carson, he'd felt... It was hard to describe. A reciprocal...awareness?

Ellery shoved his key into the stiff lock, turned it, heaved open the heavy door. He really needed to follow up with the security company and get the locks changed here as well. Maybe if he ever had a minute to spare again.

Anyway, what did it matter what Carson was trying to tell him or not tell him. After Todd, Ellery was a confirmed bachelor. Signed, sealed, and delivered. Delivered from emotional entanglements, that is. The only emotional obligation he could handle right now was a puppy, and he hadn't even managed to pull that off.

For a moment he stood in the doorway and peered into the drafty gloom waiting for him.

Then again, he was kind of tired of solitude. And celibacy.

He was building a new life for himself, and it wasn't unreasonable he might eventually want to share that life with someone. It would have to be someone from this world and not the old world, though. None of his friends and family in New York could understand why he'd felt the need to exchange the city that never sleeps for the village with narcolepsy.

And that was okay. He didn't need their understanding or approval.

He was happy with his choices. Or at least, he could envision a time when he might be happy. Presuming people stopped suspecting him of murder, the Crow's Nest started turning a profit, and he managed to find some light bulbs because holy moly, it was practically pitch-black in here!

Ellery felt around, found the light switch, but nothing happened.

Not again.

If the state of the wiring at Captain's Seat was anything like the state of the plumbing, the old mansion was probably one flick of a light switch from going up in flames. Speaking of which, he should leave one of the numerous oil lanterns and a box of matches on the table next to the front door for this kind of occasion.

Another entry for the never-ending Things to Do list that was his inheritance. Ellery suddenly remembered Tommy Rider holding a box of light bulbs, joking with him outside the hardware store. His heart sank. Such a vibrant personality. It was horrible to think she was dead. Worse. Murdered.

No. Stop. He really didn't want to let his thoughts go in that direction, or he'd back out of this spooky old mausoleum, jump in the VW, and head back to town to get a hotel room for the night. A man's home was his castle, and just because his castle was a creepy old wreck and probably haunted... just because he lived in the middle of nowhere, and the power seemed to be off, and Trevor's murderer had managed to get in here and plant that bloody sword in a hidden closet...that was no reason to start feeling unsafe in his own home.

At least the mortgage was paid off!

He listened to the surrounding darkness, trying to ignore the feeling that the darkness was listening right back at him. The tiny hairs on the nape of his neck stood up.

Ellery wavered, trying to decide what to do.

This was ridiculous, right?

It wasn't the first time the power had gone out. It wouldn't be the last.

He was exhausted, drained. That was all. His nerves were in pieces, and no wonder. He needed to get inside and go to bed.

Tomorrow he would be laughing at himself.

Hopefully not from heaven.

He reached back to pull the door shut. His heart plastered itself against his rib cage at a faint scrape of sound across the room.

"Who's there?" he demanded.

There was, of course, no answer. Because mice did not talk.

Or maybe it was a squirrel. Or a rat. Or a raccoon.

What it was not was a person in a black ski mask, holding a knife and waiting to attack him.

This. Was. Nonsense.

He pulled the door shut, slid the bolt, and started across the hall toward the staircase. He was moving briskly to prove to himself he was not afraid, but it was a mistake because the room was in almost total darkness. The only light came from one of the small porthole-shaped windows high overhead. Moonlight gilded the curved mouths of the gallery of cannons carved into the balustrade above, only to be swallowed by the darkness of the room below. Ellery's foot landed on something hard and round. He had just enough time for a disoriented flash of dismayed realization—*oh no, what's that wiffle ball doing in the hall?*—before he lost his footing.

He went down hard and hit his head on the edge of the bottom step—he had been much closer to the staircase than he'd realized. For a stunned moment he lay there blinking into the inky blackness that seemed to press in on him.

And then something stirred, moved above him on the staircase. Everything in Ellery froze. His heart seemed to ice over mid-beat. Someone turned on a flashlight and came quickly down the steps. Ellery instinctively closed his eyes, and the bright-white beam of light played across his face. The footsteps neared him, and he didn't move, didn't flinch, didn't dare to breathe. He felt the breeze of feet moving past his nose.

Beneath his lashes he saw white rubber soles and the outline of tennis shoes flash past.

The intruder sprinted for the door, slid the bolt, and shot out into the night.

* * * * *

"I don't understand," Chief Carson said, and not for the first time. "Why did you go inside the house? If you thought there was an intruder—"

"I didn't *really* think there was an intruder," Ellery protested. "I thought I was imagining things. I thought my fears were getting the better of me."

"That instinct? It's called self-preservation. You're supposed to listen to it."

Ellery retorted, "It's also called being chicken." Unlike Chief Carson, he was not raising his voice. He did not have the energy for yelling. He did not feel very well. Even though he had not been knocked out, he had received a good, hard bang on the head, and he felt a little sick and very tired. Too tired to explain that he had come home late many nights to dead light bulbs and creaky sounds and the fear that he was not alone in the mansion.

For all he knew, there had been an army of intruders wandering the house since the day he arrived, but this was the first time he'd managed to catch one.

Although *catch* was not the right word. Confirmed. That was better.

"Argh," said Chief Carson. Okay, that was not even close to what he said. What he *really* said made the paramedics blink. He finished with, "You're lucky you're not dead."

"I know."

"He's actually okay," the paramedic named Miles responded. To Ellery, he said, "You have a gash on your forehead, but it doesn't need stitches."

"Okay."

"There won't be a scar, don't worry."

Oh, right. Because everyone in Pirate's Cove apparently believed he was an actor and therefore lived in terror of a blemish. Not that he wasn't glad he wouldn't be scarred. His machismo only stretched so far.

Miles was saying, "And there's a slight possibility of concussion. I've cleaned the wound. You should try to stay awake for a few more hours."

Ellery moaned.

"Are you in pain?" Carson asked with a worried look at Miles.

"Only at the thought of having to stay awake. I'm dead on my feet."

Carson said grimly, "You came closer than I want to think about."

Miles said, "If you experience any swelling or light-headedness tomorrow, come to the med center and we'll take a closer look at you."

Ellery nodded and winced. He thanked the paramedics, who assured him it was their pleasure. They nodded good night to Carson and tromped out of the kitchen.

Ellery glanced up at Carson, and the expression in Carson's eyes made him feel suddenly, unexpectedly self-conscious. He said at random, "What *I* don't understand is why he—or she—came back here. Is it because they don't realize the sword has already been discovered?"

"I doubt it," Carson said.

"Then what?"

Carson hesitated, and Ellery realized he was trying not to dump more bad news on him in his weakened state.

He'd called Chief Carson as soon as he'd locked the door behind the intruder. Carson had shown up with his usual speed and efficiency, paramedics right behind him. He'd been flatteringly concerned when Ellery had staggered out to meet them. That had quickly given way to exasperation, following Ellery's account of the attack.

Really, you couldn't even call it an attack. Ellery had fallen over the puppy's ball without any help from the intruder. Carson hadn't believed that until he'd checked the lights in the hall and been forced to admit they had been tampered with.

"What?" Ellery insisted when Carson didn't answer his question.

Carson said quietly, "I think if my officers were to conduct a search of the house, they would find something to incriminate you in Thomasina Rider's homicide. Probably the murder weapon, since it wasn't recovered at the scene."

A wave of nausea swept over Ellery. He managed to swallow it, but his voice sounded faint to his own ears. "But I have an alibi for Tommy's murder."

"Yes. You do. An unbreakable one." Carson's smile was dour. "Our killer doesn't know that." He considered. "Maybe they don't care. Maybe the point is simply to sow confusion. Muddy the investigation as much as possible."

"Like the distraction of using an old pirate sword. There wasn't any real significance to it, but nobody could know that for sure at first."

"Exactly."

Ellery nodded and kept nodding. He was so tired, he was practically falling asleep at the kitchen table. He drank some tea—he couldn't remember who made it. Carson? The paramedics? Himself? Anyway, the brew was hot and strong and comforting.

Carson disappeared for a time and then came back. "Did you happen to leave any windows open? Any doors unlocked?"

"No way. Not after everything that's gone on." Including his own amateurish efforts at breaking into Trevor's home.

"I didn't think so. Well, you can't stay here tonight."

He didn't want to, to be honest, but Ellery asked anyway. "Why?"

"There's no sign of forced entry. I think this settles it. Your intruder has a key."

"Great." After the pirate sword had turned up in the hidden closet, he'd kind of suspected that was the case, but he'd been hoping against hope.

"Grab what you need for the night. I'll drive you into the village. You can stay at the Seacrest Inn. It's run by Nan Sweeny, Nora's niece. I've already phoned ahead."

"That's very efficient."

"Yep. That's why I'm the chief of police."

"How am I going to get my car? I'll need it to drive home tomorrow."

"We'll worry about tomorrow, tomorrow."

"Sounds like a song," Ellery murmured.

Carson's mouth twitched in the faintest of smiles. He shook his head. "You're half asleep right now. Grab your gear, and let's get going."

Ellery quickly packed an overnight bag and climbed into the passenger seat of Carson's police SUV. The radio crackled with low-volume official conversations. The interior smelled like Carson's aftershave and linen-scented Febreze air freshener. Ellery had the same vent clip in his car.

"Buckle up and put your head back," Carson ordered. Though his tone was brusque, Ellery had learned to recognize the undernote of kindness.

He obeyed, and when he next opened his eyes, the SUV was idling outside the Seacrest Inn and Nan Sweeny was coming out to meet them.

Ellery opened the car door, surprised when Carson rested a hand on his shoulder. He shot the chief a quick inquiring look, but it was impossible to read his expression in the gloom of the car's interior.

"Don't worry," Carson said. "I'm going to get to the bottom of this. Our perp doesn't know it yet, but going back to Captain's Seat tonight was a big mistake."

Ellery nodded. "Thanks."

"I promise you. Everything's going to be okay."

Nobody could make that promise with any real certainty, but if Ellery was going to believe anyone, it would be Jack Carson—because Jack Carson believed what he was saying.

"I know."

"Get some rest," Carson added. "We'll talk tomorrow."

Ellery nodded again and got out. The night air was damp and cold, and he could hear the rhythmic rush of the ocean a few yards from the inn, the distant chime of buoy bells.

"You poor thing," Nan cried, giving him a quick hug and tugging away his bag. "Here, let me take that. Come inside where it's warm. We'll get you all tucked up, safe and sound." She waved to Carson, who flashed his headlights in response before slowly pulling away from the flagstone walk.

"Thank you, that's very kind."

Tucked up safe and sound? Did she think he was twelve? But the truth was she was kind of sweet, and he was tired enough not to mind a little fussing over.

They went inside the inn, which was comfortingly warm and cozy. A fire burned cheerily in the reception area, though there was no sign of any other guests. Comfortable chairs and sofas, piled with pretty pillows, were grouped around small tables decorated with candles and jars full of sand and shells and starfish. Paintings of last century Buck Island covered the pale-blue walls.

"Gosh, what a terrifying experience for you," Nan said as Ellery signed in at the front desk.

"It's my own fault for not calling the cops the minute I felt something was off."

"Now that's very true. But nothing scares men more than looking like they're scared." She winked at him.

Ellery shook his head, but that was truer than she knew.

"Anyway, I'm so glad to finally have a chance to meet you and thank you for all you've done for Auntie Nora."

"Me doing for her?" Now that was funny. "Nora's a godsend."

Nan beamed. "I'm so glad you think so. She loves working at the bookshop. She's been so excited, she's practically walking on air." She sighed. "It's nice to have a bit of good news after all the awful things going on in this town."

"Yeah, it's a little disconcerting," Ellery agreed.

"Murder seems like something that happens to other people. To have it happen in our own hometown is unbelievable." Nan tutted softly and shook her head.

"I bet."

"Of course, you're from New York, so it's probably not quite so shocking."

"I wouldn't say that." He took the keys Nan handed over.

"I understand you're an actor as well as a bookseller. What have I seen you in?"

Ellery looked down at himself. "Kicks, jeans, jacket, sweater, T-shirt."

Nan laughed. "No, really. What movies have you been in?"

Like the night wasn't painful enough? The last thing he wanted to do was regurgitate his embarrassing film career, which had started with *Happy Halloween! You're Dead* and ended with *Happy Halloween! You're Dead 6*.

"Mostly toothpaste commercials," he said.

"You do have a beautiful smile!"

He offered a feeble version of his beautiful smile.

"I hope these terrible murders won't turn you off our little town. It's actually a wonderful place to live."

"And die," Ellery said. That was definitely the conk on his head talking.

Nan giggled. "You're bad. Janet's the one I feel terrible for."

"Janet? Why's that?"

Nan's smile was wistful. "She used to be so much fun. She was always in the thick of everything. From the Scallywags to Girl Scout troop leader. Then Trevor came along. She's like a different person now. I was hoping once they split up, it would be different, but no. I don't know how or why, but Trevor could always twist her around his little finger. Why *do* smart women make such foolish choices when it comes to men?"

In Ellery's experience, smart women were not unique in making fools of themselves over men. He said, "But their relationship had been over for a long time, hadn't it?"

"No. That is, yes, but right on schedule, Trevor started making noise about wanting to get back together. According to Janet, anyway. I tried to tell her not to trust him, but Janet had a blind spot where Trevor was concerned. Now, of course, she's devastated."

"I guess so."

Nan seemed to shake off her pensiveness. "However did we get on the topic of Janet?"

Ellery shook his head.

"Why don't you go upstairs, and I'll bring you a pot of tea? Jack said you shouldn't go to sleep right away."

"Yeah, about the not sleeping right away? I'm going to bed *now*," Ellery said firmly.

"Oh? Are you sure? Because—"

"I'm sure. Good night. Thank you for the hospitality."

"Oh, it's my pleasure. It's so nice to have company. It's like a morgue around here off-season."

"It's the nicest morgue I've ever been in," he assured her.

Nan giggled again, watching as he slowly climbed the polished wooden stairs to the corner room on the second floor. "Sweet dreams!" she called.

He was so beat, he could hardly think straight. It took all his concentration to put one foot in front of the other. Still, he felt vaguely sure Nan had said something significant during their conversation. Was it about Janet believing she was going to be getting back together with Trevor? Was it something else?

Whatever it was, it would have to wait until tomorrow.

He unlocked the door to his room and was pleasantly surprised to find it was large and lovely, with bow windows offering a view of the star-glittered sky and the lamp of the North Point lighthouse shining like a path across the bay. A green glass bowl of freshly cut lilies and lavender sat on the table near the windows, their cool, sweet perfume drifting across the room.

As Ellery undressed, he tried to convince himself he had the energy for a shower, but before he stepped out of his Levi's, he gave up the idea and fell face-first into the nest of pillows and cloudlike comforter.

Heaven.

He blinked drowsily into the soft linens. What *had* Nan said about Janet? About always being in the thick of things? About becoming a different person?

A different person...

No. It was gone now.

He summoned the strength to reach up and turn off the bedside lamp.

CHAPTER NINETEEN

"**G**ood morning, dearie! I wasn't sure we'd see you today," Nora greeted Ellery the next morning. "How are you feeling?"

"Fine. Actually, great. Your niece sure knows her way around a sausage breakfast."

Wait. That definitely sounded wrong.

Ellery hastily corrected, "Around scrambled eggs and sausages. There were even biscuits and gravy."

"Nan's a wonderful cook," Nora said proudly. "She gets that from my side of the family."

Along with her nosiness, probably, but Ellery hadn't really minded Nan's inquisitiveness. There had been no malice. She was genuinely interested in other people—and really, in these days of self-involved social media, that was kind of a nice change.

"How's the bump on your head?"

Ellery said, "I think there's a slight chance it knocked some sense into me."

Nora smiled, but her eyes were worried. "What does Chief Carson think? Was the intruder planning to kill you?"

"Probably not. He—or she—had the opportunity, and they passed."

Nora didn't look reassured, and frankly, neither was Ellery. Nora said, "I can't understand what's happened to this town. It was always so peaceful and quiet."

Trevor's what happened.

But no, that wasn't fair. It wasn't fair to blame Trevor for getting murdered. Murder could happen to anyone, as two mystery-bookstore employees could testify.

Actually, that gave him an idea...

"I think we should put our heads together and look at this situation as mystery experts," Ellery said.

"What do you mean?"

"I mean, before we get any customers, let's make a list of all our suspects and see what we come up with. I think with your knowledge of the village and my exquisite penmanship, we could solve this thing in no time."

Nora laughed and so did Ellery, but he wasn't completely joking.

"For example, if this was a mystery novel, who's our most likely suspect?"

"You," Nora answered promptly.

"*Me?*"

She considered, "Well, perhaps only in an Agatha Christie novel. But you are the least likely suspect, which makes you the *most* likely suspect."

"But I'm the hero!"

"Are you, though?"

Ellery opened his mouth, and Nora laughed. "Just teasing. I suppose Jack Carson is the most likely suspect."

"*Jack?* I mean, Chief Carson? Why?"

"I think he probably has a secret or two, don't you?" Nora was dusting the rack of bargain paperbacks in front of the counter. She didn't look at him.

"Doesn't everyone?" Ellery retorted.

She smiled, still dusting. Not that the rack really needed it. Since Nora had signed on, everything in the store was shipshape and dust-free. "Anyway, I don't believe people kill over those kinds of secrets nowadays."

Ellery said slowly, "Nora, I think you might be a witch."

She winked at him. "I would also make a good suspect. No one notices little old ladies. We can come and go, and we're practically invisible."

Ellery watched her in fascination. "But what would your motive be?"

"Something tragic in my distant past." She wrinkled her nose. "I'm not the killer, so let's not waste time on that. Who's *your* first suspect?"

"Thomasina Rider."

Nora studied him. "I see we have quite a learning curve ahead."

Ellery grinned. "I mean, she *was* one of my main suspects, but now, obviously, she's been exonerated."

"In the worst possible way."

"Yes. But." He told Nora about his conversation with Tommy the previous evening, and how it had seemed to him that Tommy had remembered something crucial to the case—only to be found dead a short time later.

"Maybe she did have a client waiting," Nora pointed out.

"Maybe. But it was like something clicked. Something to do with access to the Crow's Nest."

"Thomasina had access. She had access to any number of properties in this village. It's amazing how often people don't change their locks when they move into a new home or business."

"True." Ellery considered. "Maybe Tommy suddenly thought of someone who had access to her access."

Nora nodded. "I suppose that's possible. Yes."

"Does Tommy have a partner? Does she—did she—work in an office where anyone could walk in and grab her keys?"

"I wouldn't think so."

"Was she romantically involved? Dating anyone?"

"Probably. Usually. No one serious. Not that I heard."

And if anyone would have heard, it was probably Nora. Speaking of which.

"I just thought of another suspect," Ellery said. "My *real* suspect."

"Who?"

"The afternoon I argued with Trevor, someone was in the bookshop. I didn't see them, but they coughed. After Trevor left, I went to see who was there, but whoever it was had gone. *That* person was the sole witness to my argument with Trevor. *That* person is my main suspect!"

Ellery was having a Hercule Poirot moment, so he was nonplussed at Nora's look of horror.

"No," she said quickly. "No, you're wrong about that. That person had nothing to do with it. Nothing to do with the crime. Please believe me."

"How can you be so sure?"

Nora gulped. "Because *I* am that person!"

Perfect moment for the curtain to fall. Or the chapter to end. Art is so much more symmetrical than real life.

Instead Ellery gaped at Nora.

"What do you mean *you* were that person?"

"I'm so sorry, dearie." In her distress, Nora reached out to squeeze his hands. "I came in to see about asking you for a job, but of course it wasn't a good time. You were arguing with Trevor—really, you were trying *not* to argue with him—

so I waited a bit, but then it was obvious he wasn't going to budge, so I left."

"But…"

Nora's face screwed up as though in great pain. "And I'm such a terrible blabbermouth! I truly didn't mean to get you in trouble. I had no idea Trevor would wind up dead. So I… I mentioned to one or two friends that I'd seen you trying to fend him off, and I suppose they mentioned it to one or two friends, who mentioned it to one or two friends, and somehow it got back to Sue Lewis. I'm so sorry, Ellery. I can't *tell* you how sorry I am."

Ellery repeated slowly, "*You're* the one who started that rumor?"

It wasn't that he didn't understand. He did. He had watched her in action. Heck, a few moments ago he'd been encouraging her. But it still hurt. Thanks to Nora, Sue had been able to launch her hate campaign against him. Nora's gossiping and rumor-mongering had almost got him arrested for murder.

Watching his face, Nora probably read all that and more. She winced. "But you know, I did try to fix it. I went to Chief Carson right away and told him what I'd seen, and that it wasn't anything like Sue Lewis was making it sound. I told him she was exaggerating everything and that you had been very patient—at least for the part of the conversation I heard. As I said, I did sneak out before the end. But it was obvious you weren't about to turn homicidal."

Ellery nodded. He really couldn't think of anything to say to her.

"If you want to fire me, I understand," Nora said humbly. She wiped her eyes.

He shook his head. "I'm not going to fire you." Suddenly, their little murder game wasn't so much fun. Suddenly, he was sick of Pirate's Cove and everyone in it. "I'm going to work in my office for a while," he said.

* * * * *

A little before lunch, Chief Carson phoned and asked Ellery to come down to the police station. He sounded... formal. Formal in the way he had before they had become friends. Well, friend*lier*.

"Is everything okay?" Ellery asked tentatively. "Has something happened?"

"We'll discuss it when you get here." Carson hung up.

Naturally, Ellery's stomach was in knots by the time he walked down to the station and was directed to a wooden chair outside Carson's office.

Behind the closed door he could hear Carson talking— one voice only, so he was on the phone—but he couldn't make out the words.

It seemed to be a lengthy conversation. At last, the door to Carson's office opened. Carson said, "Come in. Have a seat."

Ellery rose and stepped inside the chief's office. He took the chair in front of Carson's desk, watching Carson go around and take his seat. Carson studied him for a moment. He looked tired and grim.

"How's the head?"

Ellery raised a hand to the strip on his forehead. "It's okay. I'm a fast healer."

Physically, anyway. Emotional wounds took longer, and he'd sustained more than a few along the way.

So much for the chitchat. Carson nodded, leaned over, pulled open a drawer, and lifted out a clear evidence bag. Inside the bag was a bloody knife—actually, it was a utility knife with a bloody blade.

Ellery couldn't seem to tear his gaze from the evidence bag.

"Recognize this?" Carson asked.

Ellery licked his lips. His mouth was suddenly dry. "No."

"I found it in the space beneath the trapdoor in your bedroom."

"I…"

Carson waited. When it was clear Ellery had nothing to add, he nodded.

"I'm confident forensic testing will prove this is the knife that killed Thomasina Rider."

"I didn't—"

"I know you didn't. You were sitting in front of me when it happened. But you can see why this situation is tricky as hell."

Yes and no. Tricky for *Ellery*, yes. No question. Carson seemed to be implying it was also tricky for himself.

"Someone is trying very hard to implicate you in these murders. What I can't understand is whether it's personal or whether it's expediency."

"Expediency?" Ellery said doubtfully.

"You're simply the easiest target. But you're not. Not really. Our killer is having to work very hard to keep the focus of the investigation on you. Going back to Captain's Seat last night was taking a big chance. Why was it worth it to take that chance?"

Ellery shook his head. "Because I *am* the most likely suspect?"

"You're not. Janet Maples is the most likely suspect and has been since the first."

Well, not the *first* first because Carson had informed Ellery he was, *of course*, the prime suspect.

"Then Janet Maples must be the killer," Ellery said.

Carson nodded, but it seemed more in agreement that this was a reasonable conclusion than that it was *his* conclusion.

"I think extra effort is being thrown in your direction because it's clear to our perp that I..." For the first time, Carson seemed less steely. "That I'm not inclined to follow this particular trail of breadcrumbs."

"Oh," Ellery said. And then his heart jumped. "*Oh?*"

"Which is a huge complication for this investigation. If I look biased, my judgment on a variety of things falls into question."

Things like whether Ellery was, in fact, the most viable suspect. He got it now.

As an aside, never had bad news felt so...good.

"Whether intentionally or unintentionally, I'm being pushed further out on a limb. If the limb breaks, we both go down."

Ellery closed his mind to inappropriate images. "Er, right."

"The fact that you were attacked by an intruder dilutes the potential damage of finding a murder weapon in your home, but it doesn't entirely get you off the hook. There were no witnesses. You could have faked the attack on yourself to divert attention."

Ellery started to respond indignantly, but Carson put a hand up.

"I don't think that's what happened. Obviously. But it's important we both understand all the possible angles."

"Okay."

"The fact that you'd have to be suicidally careless to hide the knife in your own home after the discovery of the sword isn't a guarantee that some people won't believe you really are that careless or that dumb or, possibly, suicidal. One thing about the justice system, a good lawyer can argue any side of a case, however preposterous, which is why sometimes cases are brought to trial that should never see the light of day."

Ellery suddenly understood where this was going. "You're afraid that once you let your team know where you found the knife, the investigation will be taken out of your hands."

"Yes."

"And you can't *not* let your team know because you'll be fatally compromised."

"Yes."

"I wouldn't ask or expect you to do that anyway."

"I know," Carson said. "Which is funny, given—as people will point out—I haven't known you very long."

Ellery nodded. He had no idea what to say.

"This is worst-case-scenario stuff," Carson said. "None of this may come to pass. I'm not the only witness to your being in the station at the time Thomasina Rider was killed, and it's highly unlikely that Rider was killed by someone other than the person who killed Trevor Maples. But it would be a good idea to…"

"Keep our distance?" Ellery asked wryly.

Carson sighed. "Yeah. Until the case is solved, it's probably a good idea."

They hadn't exactly been dating before. But there had been something tentative and fragile flickering between them. Carson was acknowledging it even as he painstakingly smothered it.

"Okay, I understand. I'll keep my distance. Was there anything else?"

"No," Carson said, avoiding his gaze.

Right. Because even if there was, under these new rules of engagement, Carson was not going to share any information, was not going to cross any lines.

Ellery rose. "Thank you for being honest." This was painful, but not knowing why he was suddenly being shut out would have been worse. He was grateful for Carson's directness.

Carson nodded.

"Hopefully, this will soon be..." Ellery stopped because it's not like Carson had pledged undying love or anything. In fact, it was hard to know what Carson had really been saying, other than whatever had been happening between them was on hold. Maybe for good.

"Yes, hopefully," Carson said, and looked down at the open file on his desk.

CHAPTER TWENTY

At five, a greatly subdued Nora appeared in his office.

"I was just about to close up. Did you need anything else?"

Ellery glanced up. "No. Thanks. Have a good evening."

She didn't move. "Ellery…"

Ellery sighed. "It's okay, Nora. I know you didn't mean any harm. I guess it's a little hypocritical of me to be outraged when I've been trying all week to get people to talk about Trevor and Janet and Tommy and Dylan and Cyrus and anyone else I could think of."

"I'm reforming," Nora told him. "I'm turning over a new leaf. No more telling tales out of school for me."

"Okay."

"I'm serious about this! I've learned my lesson."

Ellery grinned. "I believe you."

"You *don't* believe me, but it's true."

"How about this—every time I catch you gossiping, you put a quarter in this jar?" He picked up the vintage ceramic tree stump and pixie pencil jar, dumped the pens out, and held it up.

Nora blinked. "All right. Done." She took the holder. "I'll put this on the counter now."

"Thank you, Nora. See you tomorrow."

Ellery was smiling faintly as he heard the bell and the front door close behind her. If he was right, he'd be able to pay Nora a decent salary in no time.

He went back to the list he had been working on since returning from the police station.

SUSPECTS

DYLAN CARTER – Access to the Crow's Nest. Does he have access to Captain's Seat also? Background in theater (access to costumes and props—comfortable with a sword?). Known to have bad relations with Trevor Maples (competitors in buying theater for Scallywags). Relationship with Tommy unknown (but seems to have dated every woman in the village—access to her keys???).

CYRUS JONES – Was losing race for mayor to Trevor AND to Tommy. Argued frequently with Trevor re zoning permits, etc. HOW MUCH DID HE WANT TO WIN?????

THOMASINA RIDER – Access to everywhere and everything. Trevor's former partner in business and romance. HARD FEELINGS? Could not carry body by herself. ACCOMPLICE? Did she know too much? Trevor would trust her?

JANET MAPLES – Trevor's ex-wife. Business partner? Did she think they were getting back together? THE WIFE IS ALWAYS GUILTY. Personality changed. Used to work for police department.

Hm… Why did that seem significant now? Something Nan said last night…

Anyway.

Ellery scratched the tip of his nose with his pen. Unfortunately, so far Dylan looked like his best candidate for murderer, and Dylan was the only person he was convinced hadn't killed anyone.

Could not carry body. Trevor would trust her?

LOGAN M –

The phone rang, and Ellery absently reached for it.

"Crow's Nest."

"Ellery, this is Dr. Vincent. Imelda tells me you had second thoughts about adopting that black spaniel-mix puppy. Is that the case? Because if you want him, he's back."

"He's *back*?" It felt like someone turned all the lights on inside him. Until that moment, Ellery hadn't realized how sad he had been about losing his little partner-in-crime. "What happened?"

"It turned out not to be a good match. It was too soon. The Harmons were hoping to fill that hole in their heart left by Tootsie, but what they got was a little stranger." Dr. Vincent cleared his throat. "A little stranger who apparently never stopped barking."

In fact, Ellery could hear a tiny, shrill barking in the background.

"Yeah, I still want him. I'm on my way."

* * * * *

Fifteen minutes later, Ellery had a tiny black puppy snuffling in his neck and making almost human moans.

"He knows me!" He kissed the puppy's silky ear and beamed at Dr. Vincent and Imelda the receptionist.

"Yes, he does," Imelda said with a look of relief.

"There's no escape now," Dr. Vincent added, and he did not appear to be joking.

Ellery purchased a carrier, a bag of puppy food, and a few other necessities, which he proceeded to lug back to the Crow's Nest and his car.

He had just reached the seafront when the piercing sound of sirens filled the air.

What the—?

Sirens were not often heard in Pirate's Cove. Most residents were in good health, there was typically little crime (not including recent events), and the village was small enough that when emergencies did occur, residents could usually get the help they needed as quickly on foot—or golf cart—as by summoning official aid.

Ellery's heart stopped. His initial thought was that the bookshop was on fire. He had no concrete reason for jumping to that conclusion, but he realized now how much the anonymous note had rattled him. Unconsciously, he kept waiting for the other shoe to fall—or kick him in the teeth.

He started to run, awkwardly clutching the puppy against his shoulder, the carrier banging against his knee, but as the Crow's Nest came into view, he saw the crowd gathered on the sidewalk—mostly other shop owners working late—staring up the street in the direction of the village square.

He jogged up to Dylan. "What happened?"

"I don't know. The ambulance was pulling away by the time I got outside."

"Ambulance?"

Dylan nodded. He was staring at the puppy cuddled against Ellery's shoulder. "Did you just get a dog?"

"It's a long story, but yes. I'm adopting him." Dylan was grinning broadly. "What?"

"If you *adopted* a dog, you're here for the duration."

"Of course I'm here for the duration. I always said I was here for the duration."

"Yes, but now you're committed. There's no going back. Dogs are symbolic."

Ellery rolled his eyes. "If you say so, Mr. Ibsen." He looked past Dylan and noticed Mayor Cyrus Jones among the slowly dispersing crowd. The mayor caught his glance and made his way over.

"Shocking, isn't it?" the mayor said.

"What?" Ellery and Dylan chorused.

Cyrus announced self-importantly, "I've just been informed Janet Maples tried to kill herself."

Ellery had no idea what to say. He realized that, despite a fair bit of evidence, he had not ever really believed Janet was guilty.

"No way." Dylan looked almost angry.

"I'm afraid it's true," Cyrus insisted. "She wrote a full confession on her computer. The paramedics found it. She confessed to everything."

"What everything?" Dylan demanded.

"She confessed to killing both Trevor and Tommy."

"There is *no* way in hell she killed Tommy," Dylan said. "And I don't believe she killed Trevor." He pushed past Cyrus, making his way through the crowd. Ellery and the mayor stared after him.

Cyrus said, "Well! I had no idea he felt that way about poor Janet."

"She's part of the Monday Night Scrabblers," Ellery said.

"Of course. Of course. And she's a Scallywag. I should have thought before I spoke."

Ellery was momentarily confused, but then he remembered that the Scallywags were members of the local theater group Dylan directed.

The mayor took Ellery by the arm, guiding him toward the door of the Crow's Nest. "This is actually very good timing, dear boy. I wanted to speak to you... Oh, did you just buy a dog?"

"Sort of," Ellery admitted. "We've adopted each other." The pup yawned in his ear and tucked his head more comfortably beneath Ellery's chin.

"Isn't he adorable?" the mayor said in the polite tone of a cat person.

They reached the door of the Crow's Nest, Ellery shifted the dog and his parcels, unlocked the door, and the mayor followed him inside. Ellery dropped his purchases, set the puppy—he was going to have to come up with a name for his little buddy—on the counter. It sat up and blinked sleepily.

The mayor was saying, "I admit, Janet never seemed like the type to take her own life. She's too stubborn, for one thing, but we can't discount the evidence."

"*Was* there any evidence besides a suicide note?"

Cyrus looked startled. "Do you think more evidence would be needed?"

Well...yeah, frankly. But Ellery shrugged noncommittally. He said, "Aren't there security cameras at Old Salt Stationery?" He seemed to recall there were. In fact, the Crow's Nest was one of the only businesses in Pirate's Cove that didn't have security cameras. And knowing what he did now about the village's crime rate, that was a temporary state of affairs.

He added, "Have they recovered any of the security footage yet?"

Cyrus smiled. "Good heavens. You sound just like Chief Carson."

Ellery started to reply but was distracted by the tinkle of the bell on the front door.

Logan Maples stopped short at the sight of Ellery and the mayor. He said, "Do you know what's going on?"

Cyrus shook his head. Ellery said, "The rumor is Janet tried to kill herself."

"*What?*" Logan looked flabbergasted.

"It's not a rumor," Cyrus said. "She left a confession."

"She confessed to trying to kill herself?" Logan sounded confused.

"No, no. She confessed to…" Belatedly Cyrus seemed to remember who he was talking to. "I suppose we should wait for the official verdict."

Logan turned from Cyrus to Ellery. Ellery said, "Janet has apparently confessed to killing Trevor and Tommy Rider."

Logan's thick glasses gave him a blind look. He said, "Apparently?"

"She typed her confession on her laptop."

"Then…it's over. The case is closed."

"I don't know."

"But if she's confessed… And now she's dead too?"

"We don't have confirmation she's dead," Cyrus said.

"I thought you said—"

"She tried to kill herself. We don't know yet if she succeeded."

Logan seemed even more confused.

Ellery said, "I don't know much about suicide, but I would think most people would write out their final words."

"Nowadays they probably text them," Cyrus said. He looked promptly abashed. "Well, I should be going. I must follow up with Chief Carson on this tragic development."

"Wasn't there something you wanted to discuss?" Ellery asked.

"Oh, it can wait," Cyrus said with a meaningful look at Logan.

What did that mean? Was Cyrus also in the market to buy the Crow's Nest?

As Cyrus disappeared through the front door, Logan said, "I still can't figure out how that idiot came to be mayor."

The competition kept dying off?

Ellery held that thought to himself.

"Awful news about Janet," Logan said, approaching the counter. "I suppose she's the type, though. Hysterical. Vindictive. You said they don't don't know yet if she's going to make it?"

Maybe Janet had been vindictive. Ellery couldn't guess based on their slight acquaintance. But what she had not struck him as—not even remotely—was hysterical.

"We don't know yet."

"She must have been desperate to try something like that."

"I guess so. Did you actually know her?" Ellery asked.

"I met her a few times." Logan gave the puppy an absent pat, glancing down at the yellow legal pad Ellery had left lying there when he'd hurried out to fetch the pup from Vincent Veterinary Hospital.

Too late, Ellery remembered what was on the pad.

He watched Logan go perfectly still, watched Logan lose color, watched Logan raise his head, staring at him. "*Suspects?*" he quoted.

Well, this was awkward. Ellery felt hot with embarrassment. He opened his mouth, but Logan spoke first.

"You consider me a suspect in my own brother's death?"

"I—"

"I wasn't even here!"

"I know that. I was just—"

"You were just counting me as another suspect."

"I'm trying to work through some things in my own mind," Ellery said quickly, placatingly. "I don't really consider you a suspect. How could I? As you say, you weren't even here at the time."

"And yet I'm on the list."

"If you'll notice, I don't have anything filled in."

"Why doesn't that reassure me?" Logan said. He was scarlet with anger. "What is it you have against me, if I may be so bold?"

"Nothing. Really."

"Don't give me that. I should at least have the opportunity to defend myself."

Why, oh why had he not left that pad in his office?

"I…"

"Go on."

"Well, if I *had* to attribute a motive to you, I guess it would be something to do with gain. With Trevor owning a third of the village."

"Ha! That just goes to show what you don't know," Logan retorted furiously. "Trevor was *broke*. He was on the verge of bankruptcy. *I'm* the one with the money. *I'm* the one with the investment portfolio. I could buy and sell any one of you a dozen times over. *I* have a million dollars in my Swiss bank account. And that's just the beginning."

Yikes.

"Like I said," Ellery began, "I don't really have any—"

"No! You don't. But that doesn't stop you and everyone else from speculating. What was my reason for killing the Rider woman? I suppose I knocked her off too?"

"I never said that."

"It's implied! If I killed one, I must have killed the other."

You couldn't fault his logic.

When Ellery didn't answer, Logan said, "It's a little late for diplomacy. Go on. You must have given it some thought."

Ellery said reluctantly, "I don't know why Tommy was killed. Her relationship with Trevor must have made her privy to some information that would be dangerous to his killer."

Logan made a sound of derision. "I can't even begin to translate that babble."

Ellery said, "I already admitted I don't know why anyone would kill Tommy. Maybe she knew something she didn't know she knew."

Logan practically goggled at him. "That's it? That's your theory? That's the silliest thing I ever heard."

"You asked!" Ellery said irritably.

"I suppose you've shared all this with Chief Carson?"

Ellery said, "Chief Carson doesn't need help in his investigation from me or anyone else."

"Doesn't he? He's certainly dragging his feet on finding my brother's killer."

"Really, Logan, you're taking this *way* too seriously. I was just working a few things out in my own mind."

"So you said! What does that even mean?"

"It means *I'm* the person actually under suspicion. Well, now I guess it's Janet, but it was me. No one thinks you're involved, and you've just pointed out you had no motive, so you shouldn't—"

"Take it too seriously? If anyone ought to appreciate how it feels being unfairly suspected of murder, it's you."

Touché.

Ellery couldn't argue that one, and Logan didn't give him the opportunity. He turned, strode to the door, and shoved it open.

"And to think I was going to invite you to dine with me this evening!"

The door swung shut with a *bang*, cutting off the melodious sway of the bell.

CHAPTER TWENTY-ONE

Ellery was tempted to spend a second night at the Seacrest Inn.

Nan had the room, and she seemed like someone who would like dogs. Was there anyone who *didn't* like puppies? Last night had been the best night's sleep Ellery had enjoyed in three months, and having someone cook a hot breakfast was an added bonus.

But the very fact that he was dreading returning to Captain's Seat meant he needed to go back and face his fears. Captain's Seat was now his home. He could not afford to develop a case of the heebie-jeebies.

Anyway, after Janet's supposed suicide attempt, he was perfectly safe. Either Janet had really killed Trevor and Tommy, or she had been efficiently framed for the murders. Having successfully framed her, it would make no sense for the real killer to undo his hard work and kill again while Janet had an airtight alibi.

If it turned out that Janet had not tried to kill herself and that her confession was faked, then all bets were off. But tonight, while Janet's life hung in the balance and all of Pirate's Cove slumbered peacefully in the belief that the killer of two of their citizens was safely locked up, this was probably the safest he would ever be.

He had to hire the island's only taxi service to get him home—it seemed a lifetime ago Chief Carson had driven him to the Seacrest Inn and promised that everything would be okay—and the drive out to Captain's Seat was to the accompaniment of Ezra Christmas's theories on what would drive a woman like Janet Maples to murder.

"You don't think there's any chance she's being framed?" Ellery asked.

"Left a confession, didn't she?" Ezra pointed out. "On her own computer!"

And for all Ellery knew, Janet *had* killed Trevor and Tommy. It was hard not to hope she had, because with the suspicion lifted from him, everyone was being extra nice, no doubt feeling guilty about their previous suspicions.

Even Ezra had declined payment for the taxi ride. "We look out for our own at Pirate's Cove," he announced, waving away Ellery's bills.

Well, sometimes. And Ellery was not the type to hold a grudge.

Ellery thanked Ezra and lugged Watson—he had named the puppy on the drive from the village—and his purchases up the steps and into the mansion.

Having the pup helped. His lively, inquisitive personality—and tendency to get underfoot—kept Ellery busy for the first part of the evening. But once Watson had been played with and fed and played with some more and had finally settled down to sleep, Ellery fixed himself a Lean Cuisine Comfort Glazed Chicken and a glass of white wine and sat down to work out his doubts with a game of Scrabble.

What he'd have liked to do was phone Carson and ask him if he believed in Janet's guilt, and if he knew whether Logan Maples was as rich as he claimed, and if anyone had checked Logan's whereabouts at the time Trevor was murdered.

And while he was thinking of things to ask Chief Carson during this imaginary phone call he was never going to make, he'd have also liked to ask him if he'd been saying what he seemed to be saying that afternoon, because the more Ellery thought about it—and he had thought about it a lot—the more confused he was.

Which was kind of funny, given that Carson seemed to be a pretty direct communicator.

But seriously, what *had* Jack been trying to say?

If things had been different, Ellery would have simply called and asked him straight out. He too was a pretty direct communicator. But the one part of that conversation he had understood without qualification was to keep his distance. Certainly where the murder investigation was concerned, but also in other areas.

UNTIL FURTHER NOTICE.

That had been the message, and Ellery had received it loud and clear.

Maybe, if Janet really was guilty and the investigation was over, he and Jack—Chief Carson—might run into each other at the Salty Dog one evening and have a beer together, and who knows?

Or maybe not.

Sometimes a moment was all you got, and sometimes you didn't even get that.

Anyway, Ellery resisted the temptation to phone Carson. He ate his Lean Cuisine, had a second glass of wine, and began to sort through Scrabble tiles.

To his irritation, he got ROMANCE right off the bat (fifteen points + fifty for using all his tiles), and then JILTED (say what? fourteen points), and then nothing. Not NOTH-ING, mind you. Literally nothing. It was like the Scrabble gods were conspiring against him.

His mind wandered to the events of the day, particularly that unpleasant encounter with Logan. The more he thought about it, the more uneasy he was. Not that he didn't understand how offensive it was to be suspected of something you hadn't done, but Logan could hardly fail to notice he was last on the list of suspects—and that he was the one person Ellery had been unable to pin a motive on.

Logan had to realize everyone connected to Trevor would be considered a suspect. At least initially. So why had he gotten so bent out of shape?

Another slightly weird thing had been that tirade about all his money and wealth. If true, he really didn't seem to have any motive for wanting Trevor out of the way (even without the money and wealth, he had no discernable reason for wanting to do away with Trevor). But why was he so *angry*?

In fairness, he did come across as arrogant, egotistical, and plain-old eccentric, so maybe that was the explanation right there. Maybe it had just been an instance of *How very dare you!*

Eccentric. Yeah, Trevor had never seemed eccentric. Whereas Logan… Sometimes Logan had seemed like a person in a play. A set of mannerisms rather than a real personality.

Oh, and pressing Ellery to come up with his reasons for suspecting him in Trevor and Tommy's murders. That had felt very off. What had he been trying to prove? No, what had he been after?

Yes. That was what made Ellery uneasy. The feeling that Logan had been after something.

Ellery's next draw was COSTUME (eleven points + fifty).

The ironic thing was Logan really had nothing to gain from Trevor's death. Whereas if it had been Logan who had been murdered...Trevor would be the prime suspect. Logan's death would have solved all Trevor's financial problems.

Well, assuming there was no Mrs. Logan Maples. Assuming Logan's will still named his brother as his main beneficiary. Who would know the answer to that?

Chief Carson.

No, he definitely didn't want to ask Carson. He already knew Carson would not be pleased by signs of amateur sleuthing, let alone the implication that he needed help doing his job.

He selected another seven tiles, slid them around, studied the row of neat letters for a moment. He did not have a complete word. What he did have was that ominous prickle at the nape of his neck.

DISGUIS

Dylan did not answer his phone immediately. Ellery was pacing up and down the long entry hall when Dylan did call back.

"How's Janet?" Ellery asked.

"Alive. Barely. It's too soon to know if she's going to make it."

"I'm sorry. I know she's a friend."

"They're saying she washed down a bottle of sleeping pills with half a bottle of champagne. I don't believe it. She hated champagne. Her least favorite drink in the world."

"What if she thought she had something to celebrate?"

"She wouldn't be celebrating committing suicide, if that's your point."

"No. That's not my point."

"Sorry. I don't mean to snap. The police are hovering like they think she's going to wake up and try to make a break for it."

"Hey, kind of a weird question. Was Trevor ever a member of the Scallywags?"

The silence on the other end was blank.

Dylan said finally, "Why?"

"Just wondering. He was kind of a flamboyant personality. I could see him getting into theater."

"Yes. When he and Janet were first married, he did join the Scallywags. He quit after they split up."

Ellery's heart was pounding with excitement and alarm. Surely this was too crazy a theory. And yet...it kind of explained everything.

"Was he any good?"

"At what? Acting? Yes, Trevor was pretty good. A real ham. And it takes one to know one."

"Okay. Thanks. Dylan, if Logan tries to visit Janet, don't let him in to see her."

"Why would— What are you— Are you going to explain that?"

"Not tonight. I don't have any proof. I'll talk to Chief Carson tomorrow and see what he thinks. He's probably going to shoot me down."

"Not literally, one hopes."

"Hopefully not, but I don't think he's a big fan of helpful amateurs. Let me know how it goes with Janet."

"I will," Dylan said. "Sleep tight."

He did sleep surprisingly well at first. Maybe it was the warmth of Watson's little body curled against his back. Maybe it was the belief that he'd solved the toughest puzzle of his career. Maybe it was the knowledge that he was going to see Chief Carson to-morrow.

At some point his dreams changed, he grew restless, and the nightmares began. He was walking down the staircase, it was nighttime, and he could see someone in a pirate costume waiting for him at the bottom of the steps. As he drew closer, he saw that it was a skeleton. The skeleton drew his sword.

With a start, Ellery sat up straight in bed, his heart racing from the memory of the dream. He was drenched in sweat. The whole room felt hot.

Wait.

He sniffed, sniffed again.

Was that—?

Yes. God. It was. *Smoke.*

For one confused moment, he wondered if he could possibly be dreaming. He looked at the windows, and he could see behind the diamond panes that it was still dark outside. The stars were still shining. He hadn't even been asleep that long.

The smell of smoke was getting stronger. Heart in overdrive, Ellery half fell out of bed, taking care not to roll onto Watson, who was still fast-asleep in the tangle of blankets. He stumbled across the floor—it did not feel nearly cold enough beneath his bare feet—and wrapped his hand in his T-shirt to grab the doorknob.

The knob did not turn. It was locked. The door to his bedroom had been *locked* from the outside.

And what kind of crazy-ass security design was that? Why would anyone come up with the idea of locking a bedroom door from the outside?

Ellery tugged frantically on the knob, banged his fist against the wooden face—the heated wooden face of the door—shouted. All to no avail. No one was going to let him out. He was trapped.

And Captain's Seat was on fire.

Fear unlike anything he'd ever known swamped him. His heart was thundering, and he was breathing so fast, spots danced before his eyes. He had to fight the panic threatening to overwhelm his ability to think, to reason, to save himself.

He looked down and saw black smoke slowly unfurling beneath the door, starting to swirl around his feet.

Think.

He stumbled back to the bed, grabbed his cell phone, pressed the number for the fire department, which he had programed into the phone the first week he had moved to Buck Island. The first night he had turned a light on and the entire room had gone dark.

"Buck Island Volunteer and Rescue," an eerily calm voice answered.

He gulped out, "This is Ellery Page at Captain's Seat. The house is on fire. I'm trapped on the second floor."

"Mr. Page, we're responding to that call now. Trucks are in route. Can you get to a secure location?"

He was already at the window, peering down. He could not see anything below him, but that was good, right? No lights shining from the windows beneath him meant no fire on the ground floor?

He shoved open the window and leaned out. Cool, salty-sweet night air bathed his perspiring face and shoulders. He could taste the mist rolling in from the sea.

The voice on the phone was squawking his name, but he ignored it, sprinting to the bed and scooping up Watson, who did not appreciate being woken up from a deep slumber. He dumped his pillow out of its case, dropped the squirming puppy in, and ran back to the window.

He threw a leg over the sill and gazed down. If he had to choose, he'd prefer breaking his neck to burning to death, but mostly he'd prefer surviving the night. He could see a narrow ledge running along the side of the house. If he could safely walk along the ledge for a few feet, he'd be within within grabbing distance of one of the fifty-foot-tall red maple trees.

He leaned down, lowering the pillowcase to the ledge, then dropped down beside it, grabbing the hem just before it wiggled off the ledge. Back to the wall, he began to edge along the narrow ledge. *Step together, slide, slide.* At last he reached leafy branches. He put an arm out,, stretching as far as he could, until he was able to clamber awkwardly off the ledge onto the tree limb, which gave an alarming crack.

"It's okay, it's okay," Ellery told the dog.

By now Watson was yipping and yapping his outrage, the pillowcase bouncing wildly in Ellery's grip.

Ellery half climbed, half fell a couple of branches down, until he was able to jump down to the soft, wet grass, clutching the squirming pillowcase to his chest.

He dropped the case as he landed, and Watson scampered away, dragging the pillowcase behind him, looking like a little white ghost running for safety. The case snagged on a rosebush, and Watson vanished into the undergrowth.

For a few seconds, Ellery rested on his hands and knees, gulping in the damp night air, shaking with stress and exertion and a fair bit of shock. He still couldn't believe what had happened. Oh, he believed the house could have caught fire—he wouldn't have been surprised if it spontaneously combusted one day—but that locked bedroom door? That was something else. That was not an accident.

In the far, far distance he could hear a wail drifting on the breeze—the approach of fire engines. Thank God for that. Thank God for nosy neighbors. He shoved to his feet, straightened, and found himself gazing straight at a nightmarish figure looming out of the mist and striding toward him.

Logan.

Logan, wild-eyed, wild-haired, with black streaks like war paint over his face, coming toward him with hands outstretched like claws.

"I didn't go through all this for you to mess things up now," he growled.

Ellery knocked his hands away, tried to grab Logan and throw him to the ground. They landed in a clinch, pounding and kicking each other, rolling over rocks and sticks as they each tried for a better position.

Logan was cursing. "You couldn't leave it alone. You had to keep poking your nose in…"

Except it wasn't Logan, of course. Logan was dead. This was Trevor.

"You tried to…frame me…for murder," Ellery panted, punching at Trevor's head. He landed some solid blows, but they didn't seem to faze Trevor.

"…your own fault. I made you an offer. You should have taken it…"

An offer you can't refuse.

Trevor managed to get his meaty hands around Ellery's throat. He began to squeeze.

He was a lot stronger than he looked. His fingers locked down, crushing Ellery's windpipe, and Ellery began to kick and claw as darkness edged around his vision. The blood thudded in his ears.

No. No. Not like this.

He could hear a high-pitched shriek overhead.

Was that Trevor? Was that the blood vessels in his brain exploding? It wasn't him, because he didn't have any breath left to make a sound.

He flailed blindly, trying to find something to dislodge Trevor's killing grip. He felt over Trevor's hands, trying to tear at his fingers, then trying to jab his thumbs at Trevor's eyes, heard Trevor swearing, dimly felt blows to his face, and then just like that, Trevor's hands were yanked from his throat, Trevor was plucked off him and hurled aside. Ellery rolled onto his side, sucking in huge lungfuls of sweet, sweet oxygen.

"No you don't," Carson said. "Not this one. Not this time."

Blearily, Ellery saw Carson standing over him, braced for action. Trevor jumped to his feet, rushed toward Carson, and Carson hauled back and punched him right in the face. Trevor's whole body seemed to shudder with the force of that impact. He staggered back, sagged down to the ground, and fell forward, planting his face in the muddy grass.

Ellery managed to scramble back upright as Carson bent over Trevor, yanking his arms behind his back and handcuffing him.

Past Carson's head, he could see the firemen had already arrived, were already dragging hoses through the splintered front door of the house. He looked up and spied an unearthly red light flickering behind the windows on the second story.

No flames yet. That had to be a good sign, surely?

He looked around and realized his yard was slowly filling with police vehicles, blue and red lights cutting swaths through the misty night.

When Trevor was cuffed, Carson rose, turning to Ellery and holding out an arm in invitation. "You okay?"

Ellery nodded, stumbled forward, amazed and delighted to find himself hauled against Carson's broad shoulder and muscular chest. He could feel the hard, excited pound of Carson's heart against his own.

"I wasn't expecting you," Ellery said.

"No? I hope this isn't an inconvenience?"

Ellery let his forehead drop on Carson's shoulder. He shook his head. He could feel laughter welling in his chest, but he was afraid if he gave into it, it would turn into something else.

Carson lowered his head, lips brushing Ellery's ear. There was a hint of a smile in his voice as he said softly, "I don't ever want to—"

He broke off as a very loud and piercing sound emission reached them. On a scale of Most Annoying Noises Known to Man, it fell somewhere between giant mosquito and a jackhammer drilling into your skull.

Arf. Arf. Arf. Arf.

Arf. Arf. Arf. Arf.

ARF.

ARF.

ARF.

"Is that a dog?" Carson said wonderingly.

The barking was coming from somewhere in the overgrown flower beds. Barking? More like very irate yapping. Ellery's head jerked up. He pushed away from Carson and stumbled toward the dead rose garden.

"Watson?" he called. "Watson?"

He dropped to his knees as a small black dog burst out of the undergrowth and hurled itself into his arms.

"Hey there, buddy. You okay?"

The puppy proceeded to tell him what he thought of the nightlife in this establishment. Ellery kissed him, yelped himself as the puppy bit his nose, and then kissed Watson again.

When he glanced around, he spotted Carson talking to the fire chief. Deputies were putting Trevor into one of the cruisers.

Timing was everything, wasn't it?

He was smiling ruefully as he rejoined Carson. Carson met his eyes, smiled too, and introduced him to Fire Chief Johnson.

EPILOGUE

"**S**o Tommy must have figured out that someone was using her keys to gain access to the bookshop and Captain's Seat?"

"Trevor's not talking, but that's our best guess," Carson was saying.

"Do you think she knew it was Trevor—that Trevor was still alive?"

"I think it's likely. I think it's why she didn't immediately say what was on her mind the afternoon she spoke to you. She maybe even confronted him." Carson glanced at Ellery's half-empty mug. "Another?"

"Sure."

Carson rose, making his way through the noisy crowd to the bar. They were in the Salty Dog—a chance meeting, as it turned out—and it was the Sunday after Trevor had been caught in the act of trying to burn down Captain's Seat and murder Ellery.

Ellery glanced around the busy pub. The Fish and Chippies were onstage, performing "When I Get My Hands on You." Libby was pitching the usual Sunday night specials to the usual Sunday night crowd. Funny how fast life returned to normal. Overnight, Pirate's Cove had returned to the sleepy little village he'd known when he arrived three months ago. No more suspicious looks, no more whispers—well, fewer— no more crossing the street when he passed by. Sue Lewis had even printed a half-hearted apology of sorts in the *Scuttlebutt Weekly*.

Carson returned to the table with two frosty brimming mugs.

"When did you know Logan was actually Trevor?" Ellery asked. He'd been hoping to talk to Carson long before now, but Carson had been busy for the last couple of days, tying up the loose ends of his investigation—or maybe he just wasn't in a hurry to get together with Ellery. Hard to know with Carson.

Either way was okay with Ellery. He was attracted to Carson—maybe more than he wanted to admit—but after Todd, he wasn't in a hurry to jump into anything. Once burned, twice shy, as the saying went. That said, it had taken the difficult and dramatic events of the past week to make him realize how much he'd cut himself off from other people. Heck, he'd even been afraid to emotionally invest in a puppy—luckily, Watson was a dog who did not take no for an answer. Hiring Nora had been the first step, tomorrow night he was officially joining the Monday Night Scrabblers, and who could say what might next turn up on his social calendar.

Carson was saying, "I hate to admit it, but I didn't figure out that piece until you instructed Dylan Carter not to let Logan see Janet Maples. We already knew from the bruising on her neck and shoulders that she hadn't voluntarily swallowed that cocktail of pills and booze. Once you warned Carter, the final piece fell into place."

"You mean, you had been thinking Logan killed Trevor?"

"I was pretty sure, the last time we talked. I'd already verified that Logan was in Newport when he claimed he was out of the state. Why lie about it unless there was some reason he hadn't wanted us to know he was a ferry ride away from Pirate's Cove and his brother? There was also the fact that he and Trevor were almost identical, and yet they weren't twins, weren't even the same age. There were a lot of little things that flagged it for me."

Ellery nodded.

The Fish and Chippies finished their number and called Cyrus Jones to the stage. Cyrus got up amidst cheers and applause. He proceeded to thank Pirate's Cove for another landslide victory.

Ellery turned to make a joke to Carson, and found Carson watching him with a faint smile. Something about the look in his eyes warmed Ellery's heart.

He said at random, "If this was a mystery novel, Cyrus would have been the killer."

Carson raised his brows, sipped his brew, said, "Cyrus is pretty ambitious, but he doesn't have a mean bone in his body. That was another thing that made me wonder about our perp. There was an unnecessary…mean-spiritedness to these crimes. Mostly people kill because they feel desperate or trapped. That didn't seem to be in play."

"Yeah, that's the part I still don't understand. Why. Why did Trevor kill his own brother?"

"Money. It's that simple. Logan had it. Trevor wanted it."

"I thought they were supposed to be close."

"How close could they have been when no one but Janet had ever met Logan? No one's so busy that in ten years they can't make time to see you, unless they just don't care that much."

"How did he do it, anyway? Where did he give Logan the fatal dose?"

"Gimcrack Antiques. He doped him, dressed him in costume—Logan would have been woozy but still able to walk—then both of them staggered down the street and around the corner to the Crow's Nest. Two drunken pirates in the middle of Buccaneer's Days? Nobody thought anything of it—but we have them on security camera."

"You have them on camera?"

"Yes. It took a while to collect and sort through all the footage, but we did get them on a couple of cameras." His mouth twitched at Ellery's expression. "Sorry. But it can't all be intuition and Scrabble tiles. Sometimes you have to rely on ordinary policework."

Ellery shook his head. and took another mouthful of beer.

"But why did he go after Janet?"

"Two reasons. One, he needed a scapegoat, and you were becoming increasingly problematic in that direction. Two, one of his contacts fell out when he was over at her shop, pretending to be burying the hatchet. That naturally started Janet wondering."

"I'm glad Janet's going to be okay."

"She was lucky," Carson said. He added, "So were you."

"I know."

He said with unexpected seriousness, "When I heard that call come across the radio…those were a rough ten minutes. I didn't think we'd make it in time."

Neither had Ellery. In fact, he had not expected rescue, had not expected help. There was another lesson in there.

"Aw, shucks," Ellery said. "I'm going to start thinking you care."

"Nah," Carson said. "I just don't want to lose the only real bookstore in town. Where am I going to buy my copy of the *Scuttlebutt Weekly*?"

Ellery snorted. "Funny."

Carson grinned. He lifted his beer in a quick salute. When he lowered his mug, he said quietly, "Kidding aside, you should have let me know what you were thinking. You nearly died."

"I planned on it. I didn't realize Trevor had decided I had an expiration date. And…"

"And?"

"There was the whole distance thing."

"Distance thing?" Carson looked blank.

"Between us," Ellery reminded him. "You were worried about appearances and compromising positions."

Carson blinked. "It wasn't quite like that. And even if I had meant that, you must know I didn't mean you couldn't come to me for help."

"I'm the self-reliant type," Ellery said. He was kidding, but it was true. Not always smart, but true.

"Anyway, the investigation is over, so the Distance Time Speed formula no longer applies."

"No?"

"No."

"Honestly," Ellery said. "I didn't think you liked me much. Anytime I caught your eye in here you were always watching me, like you didn't trust me."

Carson gave him a funny smile. "It wasn't that. You were just very…watchable." He added gravely, "I used to really enjoy those toothpaste commercials."

Ellery groaned and then laughed.

Carson laughed too.

Ellery shrugged. "I guess the only remaining mystery is who sent me that poison pen letter."

"I'm sorry to say I don't have the answer to that one." Carson tilted his head, studying him. "That's not the only mystery though."

"No?"

"No."

Carson's smile was quizzical, and once again, Ellery felt that unexpected warmth in his chest. He asked very innocently, "What mysteries remain, Chief?"

"You're not going to make this easy, are you?"

Ellery studied him back. He smiled. "Nope."

SECRET AT
SKULL HOUSE

Ellery Page is back—and poking his elegant nose into trouble again!

Unlike everyone else in Pirate's Cove, Ellery Page, aspiring screenwriter, reigning Scrabble champion, and occasionally clueless owner of the village's only mystery bookstore, is anything but thrilled when famed horror author Brandon Abbott announces he's purchased legendary Skull House and plans to live there permanently.

Ellery and Brandon have history. Their relationship ended badly, and the last thing Ellery wants is a chance to patch things up—especially when his relationship with Police Chief Jack Carson is just getting interesting. But then, maybe Brandon isn't all that interested in getting back together either, because he seems a lot more interested in asking questions about the bloodstained past of his new home than discussing a possible future with Ellery. What is Brandon really up to?

Ellery will have to unscramble that particular puzzle posthaste. Because after his former flame disappears following their loud and public argument, Ellery seems to be Police Chief Carson's first—and only—suspect.

AUTHOR'S NOTE

Dear Reader,

Welcome to Pirate's Cove, where dark secrets lie buried in pretty window boxes and the cobbled streets run red with blood. JUST KIDDING. *Murder at Pirate's Cove* is the first book in the new M/M cozy mystery series Secrets and Scrabble. As with all cozy mysteries, there is no on-screen violence or sex, and the cursing must be minimal, damn it. There are no politics in this world. According to the rules of the game (by *game*, I mean the cozy genre not Scrabble) the stories are quick, light, and fun. While there may be (and there is) a romantic subplot, these stories are first and foremost mysteries. This may not be your cup of tea, but in these trying times, I find myself turning more and more often to the reassuring comfort of frequent murder in a world where justice always prevails and good will triumph.

The stories are set on fictional Buck Island. The character of Watson is based on my own newly adopted pup Spenser (formerly known as Watson).

Thank you to Keren. You are a lifesaver. Thank you to Kevin. You're not so bad yourself.

ABOUT THE AUTHOR

Author of over sixty titles of classic Male/Male fiction featuring twisty mystery, kickass adventure, and unapologetic man-on-man romance, JOSH LANYON'S work has been translated into twelve languages. Her FBI thriller *Fair Game* was the first Male/Male title to be published by Harlequin Mondadori, then the largest romance publisher in Italy. *Stranger on the Shore* (Harper Collins Italia) was the first M/M title to be published in print. In 2016 *Fatal Shadows* placed #5 in Japan's annual Boy Love novel list (the first and only title by a foreign author to place on the list). The Adrien English series was awarded the All Time Favorite Couple by the Goodreads M/M Romance Group. In 2019, *Fatal Shadows* became the first LGBTQ mobile game created by Moments: Choose Your Story.

She is an Eppie Award winner, a four-time Lambda Literary Award finalist (twice for Gay Mystery), An Edgar nominee, and the first ever recipient of the Goodreads All Time Favorite M/M Author award.

Josh is married and lives in Southern California.

Find other Josh Lanyon titles at www.joshlanyon.com, and follow Josh on Twitter, Facebook, Goodreads, Instagram and Tumblr.

For extras and exclusives, join Josh on Patreon.

ALSO BY JOSH LANYON

NOVELS

The ADRIEN ENGLISH Mysteries

Fatal Shadows • A Dangerous Thing • The Hell You Say
Death of a Pirate King • The Dark Tide
So This is Christmas • Stranger Things Have Happened

The HOLMES & MORIARITY Mysteries

Somebody Killed His Editor • All She Wrote
The Boy with the Painful Tattoo • In Other Words...Murder

The ALL'S FAIR Series

Fair Game • Fair Play • Fair Chance

The ART OF MURDER Series

The Mermaid Murders •The Monet Murders
The Magician Murders • The Monuments Men Murders

The SECRETS AND SCRABBLE Series

Murder at Pirate's Cove

OTHER NOVELS

The Ghost Wore Yellow Socks
Mexican Heat (with Laura Baumbach)
Strange Fortune • Come Unto These Yellow Sands
This Rough Magic • Stranger on the Shore • Winter Kill
Murder in Pastel • Jefferson Blythe, Esquire
The Curse of the Blue Scarab • Murder Takes the High Road
Séance on a Summer's Night
The Ghost Had an Early Check-Out

NOVELLAS

The DANGEROUS GROUND Series
*Dangerous Ground • Old Poison • Blood Heat
Dead Run • Kick Start • Blind Side*

The I SPY Series
*I Spy Something Bloody • I Spy Something Wicked
I Spy Something Christmas*

The IN A DARK WOOD Series
In a Dark Wood • The Parting Glass

The DARK HORSE Series
The Dark Horse • The White Knight

The DOYLE & SPAIN Series
Snowball in Hell

The HAUNTED HEART Series
Haunted Heart Winter

The XOXO FILES Series
Mummie Dearest

OTHER NOVELLAS
*Cards on the Table • The Dark Farewell •The Darkling Thrush
The Dickens with Love • Don't Look Back • A Ghost of a Chance
Lovers and Other Strangers • Out of the Blue
A Vintage Affair • Lone Star (in Men Under the Mistletoe)
Green Glass Beads (in Irregulars) • Blood Red Butterfly
Everything I Know • Baby, It's Cold • A Case of Christmas
Murder Between the Pages • Slay Ride*

SHORT STORIES

A Limited Engagement • The French Have a Word for It
In Sunshine or In Shadow • Until We Meet Once More
Icecapade (in His for the Holidays) • Perfect Day
Heart Trouble • In Plain Sight • Wedding Favors
Wizard's Moon • Fade to Black • Night Watch
Plenty of Fish • The Boy Next Door
Halloween is Murder

COLLECTIONS

Stories (Vol. 1) • Sweet Spot (the Petit Morts)
Merry Christmas, Darling (Holiday Codas)
Christmas Waltz (Holiday Codas 2)
I Spy...Three Novellas
Point Blank (Five Dangerous Ground Novellas)
Dark Horse, White Knight (Two Novellas)
The Adrien English Mysteries
The Adrien English Mysteries 2